Leonardo Padura was born in Havana in 1955 and lives there with his wife Lucía. A novelist, journalist, and critic, he is the author of several novels, one collection of essays and a volume of short stories. His *Havana* series crime novels featuring the detective Mario Conde, published in English by Bitter Lemon Press, have been translated into many languages and have won literary prizes around the world. Padura's recent novels, *The Man Who Loved Dogs* and *Heretics*, have cemented his position among the best authors in world literature. In *Grab a Snake by the Tail*, Padura returns to his roots as a crime writer, taking his hero, Police Lieutenant Mario Conde, into the dark and dangerous streets of the Barrio Chino, Havana's Chinatown.

ALSO AVAILABLE
FROM BITTER LEMON PRESS
BY LEONARDO PADURA

The Man Who Loved Dogs

Heretics

Havana Red

Havana Black

Havana Blue

Havana Gold

Havana Fever

GRAB A SNAKE BY THE TAIL

Leonardo Padura

Translated by Peter Bush

BITTER LEMON PRESS
LONDON

BITTER LEMON PRESS

First published in the United Kingdom in 2019 by
Bitter Lemon Press, 47 Wilmington Square, London WC1X 0ET

www.bitterlemonpress.com

First published in Spanish as *La cola del serpiente* by
Tusquets Editores, S.A., Barcelona, 2011

Bitter Lemon Press gratefully acknowledges the financial
assistance of the Arts Council of England

© Leonardo Padura, 2011
English translation © Peter Bush, 2019

A CIP record for this book is available from the British Library

Paperback ISBN 978–1–912242–17-7
Ebook: ISBN 978–1–912242–18-4

Typeset by Tetragon, London
Printed and bound by CPI Group (UK) Ltd, Croydon, CR0 4YY

Supported using public funding by
ARTS COUNCIL
ENGLAND
LOTTERY FUNDED

To Lydia Cabrera, for the *ngangas*.

To Francisco Cuang, for San Fan Con.

To Lucía, who understands me even when I speak in *chino*.

A chino fell down a well,
his insides turned to water...

CUBAN NURSERY RHYME

Author's Note

In 1987, when I was working as a journalist on the evening paper *Juventud Rebelde* [*Rebel Youth*], I carried out detailed research in order to write an article on the history of Havana's Barrio Chino. That text, titled 'Barrio Chino: The Longest Journey', soon became the subject of a short film documentary (*El viaje más largo*, directed by Rigoberto López), and the articles I wrote for that newspaper and which I published in book form in 1995 shared their names with the documentary.

The mysteries of the Barrio Chino and its history of loyalty to and uprooting of specific traditions had intrigued me so much that – after I'd created the character of Mario Conde and published his first two stories, *Pasado Perfecto* (1991) [*Havana Blue*, 2007] and *Vientos de cuaresma* (1993) [*Havana Gold*, 2008], I wrote a piece of fiction set in that neighbourhood of Havana. The short story also features Conde as its main character, but from a literary point of view it falls outside the four novels that comprise the Havana quartet, which was completed in the following years with *Máscaras* (1997) [*Havana Red*, 2005] and *Paisaje de otoño* (1998) [*Havana Black*, 2006].

However, I never felt the story was finished until, after I'd completed and published the last volume of the quartet,

I decided to go back and transform it into a novella. As with all of Conde's adventures, what is narrated is fiction, though there is a strong element of reality. Here, behind the police business that pulls Mario Conde towards the Barrio Chino, is the history of an uprooting I have always felt very moving: that of the Chinese who came to Cuba (originally with labour contracts that almost reduced them to a state of slavery), similar to so many economic migrants in today's world. Loneliness, contempt and uprooting are then the subject of this story that didn't really take place, but could quite easily have done.

The novella, written in 1998, was published in Cuba – where the opportunities to publish must be grasped whenever and however they appear – as a companion to another volume, *Adiós, Hemingway*.

Twelve years later, when I finally decided to hand over *La cola de la serpiente* to my Spanish publishers, the fate of this text underwent another twist: it was clear the plot's treatment was too restrictive, while several characters and situations needed greater development and the writing loosening up so it would be more in line with other works featuring Mario Conde as hero.

What you are about to read is the result of this new and, I hope, last rewrite of a story that, over fifteen years, has pursued me until it became this short novel which, I repeat, I hope has finally found its definitive form. In the end, perhaps it couldn't have happened differently, since, when writing this last version, I realized that possibly none of the Chinese community whose lives and fates inspired this work are left in Havana.

Mantilla, January 2011

1

From the moment he started to reason and learn about life, as far as Mario Conde was concerned, a *chino* had always been what a *chino* ought to be: an individual with slanted eyes and skin which, despite its jaundiced yellow colour, was able to withstand adversity. A man transported by life's challenges from a place as mythical as it was remote, a misty land amid tranquil rivers and impregnable, snow-peaked mountains, lost in the heavens; a country rich in legends about dragons, wise mandarins and subtle sages with good advice on every subject. Only several years later did he learn that a *chino*, a genuine, real *chino*, must also be a man capable of conceiving the most extraordinary dishes a civilized palate dare savour. Quails cooked in lemon juice and gratinéed with a ginger, cinnamon, basil and cabbage sauce, say. Or pork loin sautéed with eggs, camomile, orange juice and finally browned slowly in a bottomless wok, over a layer of coconut oil.

However, according to the limited ideas that derived from Conde's historical, philosophical and gastronomic prejudices, a *chino* might also be a lean, affable character ever ready to fall in love with mulatto and black women (provided they were within reach), and puff on a long, bamboo pipe with his eyes shut and, naturally, the laconic kind who utters the minimum words possible in that sing-song, palatal language they employed when speaking the languages other people speak.

"Yes, a *chino* is all that," he muttered after a moment's thought, only to conclude, after longer ruminations, that such a character was simply *the* standard *chino*, constructed by stereotypical Western thinking. Even so, Conde found it such an appealing, harmonious synthesis he wasn't too concerned if that familiar, almost bucolic image would never have meant a thing to a real live *chino*, let alone to someone who didn't know and, naturally, had never enjoyed the good fortune to taste the dishes cooked by old Juan Chion, the father of his friend Patricia, who was directly to blame for the fact that Conde had now been forced to reflect on his poor level of knowledge of the cultural and psychological make-up of a *chino*.

His need to define the essence of a *chino* had been prompted that afternoon in 1989 when, after many years without venturing into the rugged terrain of Havana's Barrio Chino, the lieutenant revisited those slums, following the call of duty: a man had been murdered, though, on this occasion, the deceased was indeed Chinese.

There were complications, as there almost always are in situations involving a *chino* (even when the *chino* in question is dead): for example, the man, who turned out to be one Pedro Cuang, hadn't been killed in the run-of-the-mill way people were usually killed in the city. He hadn't been shot, stabbed, or had his head bashed in. He hadn't even been burned or poisoned. In terms of the deceased's ethnic origins, it was a strange, far too recherché oriental murder for a country where living was considerably more taxing than dying (and would be so, for some time): one could almost call it an exotic crime, seasoned with ingredients that were hard to digest. Two arrows etched in his chest with the blade of a knife, and a severed finger to add extra flavour.

Several years later, when Mario Conde was no longer a policeman, let alone a lieutenant, he was forced to revisit Havana's Chinatown to investigate an obsession he couldn't get out of his mind, the mysterious disappearance of bolero singer Victoria del Rio in the 1950s. When he returned, he would find a more dilapidated neighbourhood that was almost in ruins, besieged by refuse collectors who couldn't cope and delinquents of every colour and stripe: the fifteen years between his two incursions into that area had sufficed to obliterate most of the old character of a Barrio Chino that had never been particularly elegant; all that was left to mark it out from the city's fifty-two official districts was its name and the odd illegible, grimy noticeboard identifying an old company or business set up by those emigrants. And if you really persevered, you might come across four or five cardboard *chinos*, as dusty as forgotten museum pieces: the last survivors of a long history of coexistence and uprooting who acted as the visible relics of the tens of thousands of Chinese who had come to the island throughout a century of constant migrations and who had once given shape, life and colour to that corner of Havana …

It was precisely on the day of his return to the area that a now older, more nostalgic Conde began to reminisce, in unlikely detail (given his increasingly poor state of recall), about that morning in 1989 when he had decided to wallow in solitude and the pages of a novel and was disturbed by the sudden appearance of Lieutenant Patricia Chion's exuberant anatomy, on a friendly rather than professional errand, a request that would make Mario Conde's existence even more stressed and challenge all the stereotypical notions about *los chinos* he had happily cherished hitherto without ever bothering to commit them to paper.

At the end of many a sweaty day in Chinatown, the most painful part for Conde would be his realization that the typical, exemplary *chino* of his imaginings would become an unfathomable being plagued by open sores, like the deep waters of a sea that vomited up old, still lacerating stories of revenge, ambition and loyalty along with the bubbles from so many frustrated dreams: almost as many as the Chinese who came to Cuba.

Honestly, it really was worth stopping and taking a long look. And his initial impression was that there was nothing pure about that prime specimen of a woman standing in front of him. His second conclusion was that the result of this obvious impurity surpassed any art created by human hands.

When he saw her, Conde remembered the conveniently forgotten saga of the failure of the F-1, that socialist Cuban miracle of livestock production (one of so many miracles that evaporated), the perfect animal that would derive from the coupling of choice specimens from the Dutch Holstein breed – a great milk producer but short on meat – and the tropical Zebu, not given to lactation but nevertheless a wonderful supplier of steak. Naturally, the F-1 would take the best from the genes of both its creators and, by dint of a simple, if ingenious, method of addition and subtraction, a single beast would be generated that would provide milk and meat in abundance. As the whole process appeared so easy and natural, there would soon be so many well-endowed cattle in Cuban dairies that the island might be flooded in milk (as Conde remembered perfectly, great leaders had promised in enthusiastic speeches that by 1970 butter and milk would be on sale and there'd be no need to produce ration books), with the danger that Cubans might even choke on their huge steaks or suffer perilous levels of cholesterol, calcium and uric acid … But life had demonstrated that F-1s needed much more than fiery orators and long-gloved inseminators, so there were no F-1s, or milk, butter and beefsteaks … not even mince. There were none in 1970 and they still hadn't surfaced, and as a result (collateral effect) acceptable levels of cholesterol had been maintained, together with rather low levels of haemoglobin.

Conversely, Patricia Chion was an F-1 created from the purest *chino* and the blackest black. That highly satisfactory mix, with equal ratios from both genes, had given the world a Chinese mulatto who was five foot seven with the blackest hair that descended in rebellious but gentle ringlets, the owner of perversely slanted (almost murderous) eyes, a petite mouth with thick lips brimming with succulence, and magnetic, smooth milk-chocolate skin.

Those delights were enhanced by other eye-catching features: small, scandalously pert breasts, a narrow waist that flared into immense round hips that flowed into the immeasurable heights of her buttocks, amounting to one of the most exultant asses in the Caribbean that melted into powerful thighs and reached a tranquil haven of vein-free legs flexed by small muscles. The whole ensemble cut breath short, made pulses race and filled heads with evil thoughts and desires (*fuck that; they're not evil, they're wonderful!*).

But she didn't merely merit a passing glance, like a painting in a fine museum. That woman attracted you like La Gioconda, or, better still, like the hottest (and best) version of Goya's Duchess of Alba: a police lieutenant specializing in financial crime, Patricia Chion liked being teased, relished displaying her charms, aided and abetted by a blouse button opened over her cleavage and a skirt always inches shorter than regulations stipulated, ploys that, with her way of walking, pointed to a Caribbean rather than Asian character. Her body and mind transformed an anodyne police uniform into temptation, as some nurses do. Conde had counted on that morning being routine leisure time, but, on his doorstep, he now gaped, as ever, at the sweet sight of F-1 and gave his wicked thoughts free rein.

"That will do, Mayo," Patricia said, using her personal nickname for Mario Conde, ending his period of rapt contemplation and rewarding him with a loud kiss on the cheek.

"So what brings you here?" he asked, once he could breathe, swallow and speak again.

"You planning to keep me in the doorway?"

Conde finally acted.

"I'm sorry, hell, the truth is …" He moved away from the door. "Come in, and please ignore the mess … I was going to give the house a clean today. As I'm on holiday and …" His nerves on edge, Conde continued lying shamelessly.

When she walked past and kissed his cheek, Patricia's smell hit Conde: clean skin, a healthy body, and, basically, a woman. And that was why he felt a real desire to cry as she walked across his living room …

"A man, and a policeman to boot: always bad news for a house … But I've seen worse dens," Patricia admitted, as she stopped in the middle of the room and glanced back at Conde. "You know me, I'll offer you a deal."

Conde smiled. And let himself be tempted. Naturally, he would happily have been dragged into hell provided Patricia was holding his hand.

"I know you're going to fuck me up, but … what's all this about?"

"If you delay your vacation and take on a case, I'll help you clean your house."

Conde anticipated that the way he answered those words would cost him much more than he could imagine, but he had no choice. Jettisoning all his steely resolutions about not doing anything on his free days, he said: "All right … what's this case about?"

Patricia smiled, put her briefcase on a pile of magazines gathering dust on an armchair, rummaged in her bag and extracted a hairband. She deftly gathered her black ringlets and bunched them at the back of her neck.

"Lend me some shorts and an old jersey and I'll tell you while we're cleaning …"

Patricia took off her shoes, levering one with the heel of the other and, now barefoot, opened the third button of her blouse. Meanwhile, Conde's legs began to tremble and he felt a drop of lubricant slip down his urethra.

"Hey, Mayo, I'm not doing a striptease, give me some clothes … and make sure they're clean," demanded Patricia, and in the end the cop reacted.

Two hours later the house was as clean and tidy as they could have hoped for in the time they'd had. Mario Conde was simultaneously brought up to date on the scant information that existed about the murder of one Pedro Cuang. Above all, he discovered why Patricia wanted him: according to her, it would be impossible to solve that case without a trustworthy guide in Chinatown. And Patricia knew that out of all the detectives at Headquarters Conde would have some chance of getting to the truth because of his friendship with her own father, Juan Chion.

"Besides, the victim was a friend of my godfather, Francisco … and I'm sure my dad knew him, even if he told me otherwise."

"And before you talked to me, did you ask your father to help me?"

"Come on, Mayo, the moment I decided to come and see you, I knew you were never going to say no … Otherwise, why are we friends?"

And even if she didn't have enough strength to disarm him, Patricia's voice, when she adopted that half-imploring, half-vampy tone, was capable of stripping Conde of everything. Down to his underpants.

While he drank his second cup of coffee in the kitchen, Mario Conde listened to the shower water splashing off Patricia Chion's naked body. Luckily, two days earlier he'd been round at Skinny Carlos's place and had put several towels and sheets in Josefina's – his friend's mother's – washing machine, and was able to offer Patricia reasonably clean towels when she said she couldn't go back to work in the state she was in after they'd finished their cleaning blitz. Although Conde could have gobbled her up with any number of layers of grime, he made a final effort, the supreme one of that morning, and said goodbye to Patricia from the kitchen once she was in the bathroom, behind a closed door and, ever a cautious *china*, with the bolt on. His mind racing, Conde smoked in the kitchen, ears attuned to the sound of water streaming down her body and imagining the rivulets that lucky water was creating on her cinnamon skin.

Half an hour later, while preparing to have a shower before leaving to find ways to fulfil his side of the deal with Patricia Chion, Conde spotted a thick, black hair in the tub; it was curled in on itself, like a spring, a hair that could only be one of the *china*'s pubic hairs. With her bush in his eyes and dizzy from the clean-woman smell still floating in the bathroom, he made his mind up and sat on the edge of the tub. He didn't put up much of a fight; after all, he had only a single source of relief for his longings within reach.

2

It was that same night, on a packed and noisy bus en route to Juan Chion's house across a dark, torrid and increasingly aggressive city, that Mario Conde started to pull together his threadbare ideas about the make-up of a *chino*. But after fine-tuning his model with all the experiences he could channel, it was obvious he had only managed a pathetic, rather pitiful schema. "If Mao Tse-tung hears me or Confucius grabs me ..." the then lieutenant muttered, thinking that the Long March, the Cultural Revolution, even the Great Wall of China, the enormous mythological dragons and other phenomena from that larger-than-life country could never have been generated by that modest *chino* endowed with a culinary gift for inventing dishes. In the end, though, he wasn't as appalled by his transformation of a man as upstanding as Juan Chion into his stereotype. The old man deserved as much and, besides, Conde had discovered that the exercise of trying to discover what constitutes a *chino* in a clammy, stinking, overcrowded bus had notable pluses: you stopped worrying about being brushed by undesirable appendages and even about somebody taking the seat yours truly had a right to when the black built like a bricklayer got up to get off and a busty mulatta thrust a tit into the space and shattered the just aspirations of Conde, ever a man who loved to sit on a bus, face the window and, from a decent height, look out for fronton courts, towering arches and tall shrubs in places that, at ground level, remained out of sight.

The only irresistible feelings at that hour, even for someone travelling in a packed, sweaty bus, were hunger pangs: Juan Chion and food had become so intertwined that the mere thought he was heading to the old man's house started a rumble in his belly that was always ready to welcome concoctions that, miraculously, always tasted delicious. Aubergines stuffed with duck boiled in a bamboo and purslane sauce, sprinkled with crunchy mashed peanut ...

Mario Conde alighted from the bus at the stop on Infanta and Estrella, and to get his feet on the sidewalk he almost had to hurl himself against the hordes trying to get on at the same time.

"Out of the way, saggy bum, a bus ain't no bed," said the woman, elbowing him as she pushed past, and Conde didn't even feel the need to answer back. *I'm a saggy bum, am I?* he wondered, and stood and watched the vehicle judder off, bellowing menacingly, shrouded in a cloud of black smoke as if its inevitable destination was hell itself. Then he patted his sweat-stained shirt, eased his pistol against his belt and started to walk the three gloomy blocks to the home of Juan Chion and Lieutenant Patricia Chion in old Calle Maloja.

He soon forgot the busty mulatta and her insult, because the din in the street was a thousand times worse than the bus's hostile, crammed promiscuity. *What the hell was all that, a carnival or a demonstration?* he asked himself, venting his anger at the absurdity of such an impossible notion: there were no longer carnivals or spontaneous demonstrations in Havana (no matter what the ever-euphemistic newspapers kept saying), though there certainly were endless daily blackouts and high temperatures for May. Conde would have preferred to walk aimlessly, without rushing, along an empty street, thinking whatever his brain was in the mood to think, since, basically, he was only a melancholy memory man, as his friend Skinny Carlos liked to say. But in the heat of the night, aggravated by an irritating blackout, every denizen of that central district seemed to need the air in the street to survive, and a bustling throng had overflowed from sidewalks onto the asphalt, lugging kerosene lamps as well as stools, benches, beds and domino tables, and even the odd bottle of rum in order to await the return of their electricity in the best manner possible.

"Who the hell do those bastards think they are? How fucking long are we going to be without light?" shouted someone peering over a balcony, and a murmur of approval spread along Calle Maloja, ending the resigned spirit of that obligatory collective vigil.

Accustomed to waiting eternally, those people remembered now and then that you *could* make demands, although they didn't know how or where. Then Conde hurried along and blessed his habit of never wearing a police uniform. Over the last few months the blackouts, caused by the sporadic delivery of Soviet oil, had led to bottle-throwing in the streets, the breaking of shop windows and other spontaneous acts of vandalism, which was why he was so relieved to hear the contented mutterings when light finally came back as the power was restored.

Like animals trained to respond to orders, people shouted: "About time too!", "Just as well!", "Hey, today's episode is about to start!" and vacated the street in under a minute, switching on fans, lights and televisions to reveal, in the flickering illuminations from a couple of bulbs on each street corner, the intrinsic ugliness of that modest, proletarian district on its road to ruin, a district which didn't even enjoy the benefit of the occasional tree to enliven the panorama.

Juan Chion's house had a door and two large windows overlooking the street, and when visiting, Conde always felt it was being crushed by the two adjacent houses. All the buildings in the block were high and dated from 1910 to 1930, and for years they'd been crying out for refurbishment and licks of paint to postpone the threatening apocalypse. It was in that quintessential Havana street, where in colonial times they had sold the maize that gave the street its name, that Alejo Carpentier said he was born, and a few years later, when Conde discovered that the writer's birth in the city was more fictional than real, he granted that the creator of those fictions had been clever to choose, from the many possibilities, a street sufficiently anonymous and at the same time so genuinely Havanan to transform an F-1 with a French father and Russian mother into the purest Havanan.

The bronze knocker clattered against the black wooden door and Juan Chion's smile made up for the handshake that a *chino* never gave.

"Conde, Conde, so good to see you," said the old man, greeting him with a quick bow and ushering him into the house.

"By any chance did you ever build the Great Wall of China, Juan?" he asked, and smiled at his host's bemused expression at that bizarre question. "But don't worry about that, tell me, how are you?"

"All 'light," responded the old man, offering him a seat while he sat in a shabby armchair that despite Patricia's beseeching he had not turned into rags and lumber to put in the garbage can. The *chino* adored that armchair, which had a special value for him: his wife had bought it for two pesos in a second-hand store on Calle Muralla run by Polish Jews and, after reupholstering it with brocaded material, she had given him it as a birthday present in 1946, several years before Patricia was born. "Me feel fine, Conde, exercises good for you, you know. T'ai chi …"

Conde lit a cigarette and nodded. He couldn't remember the last time he'd had any repeated exercise apart from the one he'd just practised at midday sitting on the rim of his bathtub.

"Where's your daughter? Isn't she back yet? … She said we'd probably see each other here tonight."

That was when Juan Chion stopped smiling, but only for a second. He could say the most terrible things in between smiles.

"Is c'lazy, Conde, talk to her. Has got this ve'ly young man and she's c'lazy. Gets back ve'ly late eve'ly night."

Mario Conde decided he was an unlucky man and Patricia was evidently a frenzied nymphomaniac and bitch. It now transpired a young nobody was enjoying Patricia's multiple bodily charms. The worst of it was that Conde had joked to Lieutenant Patricia for years, making it plain he might be totally serious, that his lifelong dream was to lay a Chinese mulatta with a really big ass. Then, in the manner of his Grandfather Rufino's roosters, he would strut around her as if still needing to prove that Patricia might be a good candidate. The *china*, like the bitch she was, always laughed and said that one day he'd probably get what he wanted, and Conde implored her: "The sooner, the better ..." But now, after putting on one of Conde's jumpers, after cleaning Conde's house barefoot and showering stark naked in his house, she was out gallivanting with a young lad. *What a bitch*, he thought, and tried to find immediate relief for his genuine angst.

"Juan, you got any rice wine left?"

"Hang on, Conde, hang on," the old man repeated, waving to him to be patient. "Me made you tea. G'leen tea, from Canton. If you d'link it ve'ly hot, it cool you down ..."

"But don't you have any wine? What about some sake?"

Juan Chion didn't reply; instead he got up and levitated into the kitchen like a cosmonaut. Lieutenant Mario Conde thought that a drop of strong rice wine or a cup of sake (it didn't matter if it wasn't Chinese, the important thing was the degree of alcohol) would have been better than a cup of tea to get Patricia Chion and her envied young man out of his head and remind Juan Chion that he wasn't there simply to slurp egg and pigeon soup seasoned with the countless herbs Juan Chion had recited down the telephone, but also because a fellow countryman of his, the friend of another countryman of his, had died in the strangest circumstances and, as Patricia had forewarned him and he had experienced in practice, he needed the old man's help to get into the underbelly of Chinatown. And then, if he could, he'd find out why they had killed that old *chino*.

"The forensics have finished working on the body. We were waiting for you before removing it because I wanted you to see how they found him. I'll tell you now, this is a very peculiar business," Manolo had said when he saw him arrive in the afternoon, and Mario Conde couldn't understand why the sergeant's patter was making him so cheerful. Perhaps because it was good to have something different on your hands now and then? It made a change from the same thieves, the same fraudsters, the same bastards getting rich from their positions of power; the same double-crossing can get boring, and a dose of something extraordinary – or exotic – works wonders for a policeman's routine.

"So what's so peculiar, Manolo?"

"Just take a look," Sergeant Manuel Palacios had replied with a characteristic dramatic flourish, pointing out the route from the street to the room in the tenement where the crime had taken place. Conde had prepared himself: he'd been in the police for ten years, but a case involving *chinos* had never come his way.

"Juan, you don't mind if we call you *chinos chinos* now, do you?" Conde began, holding a cup of boiling, highly scented tea and becoming far too garrulous because he was feeling out of sorts sexually. "It's not offensive, is it? Because *chinos* are *chinos*, though you mustn't call *negros negros*, even if they're blacker than the backside of a turkey buzzard. Well-brought-up children are taught to say 'a person of colour', but that's because they're black, right? My grandad, Rufino, used to tell me to call them 'darkies'. I'm part black, you know? On the side of my father, my mother, or the Holy Ghost … Well, to get to the point, they've never killed a *chino* on my turf and ever since I saw him this afternoon, I've been thinking in *chino* …"

Sergeant Manuel Palacios hadn't exaggerated at all: the man had lived on Calle Salud, almost on the corner with Manrique, in the very heart of the Barrio Chino, and the first thing that shocked Conde was the huge number of *chinos* gathered in the passage in the rooming house. They had been crouching silently, like sparrows perched on a wire, and all had stared at the policeman when he walked in. Their way of looking had been oblique, ponderous and grief-stricken and had stirred the feelings of the lieutenant detective, who would always remember thinking: "It's like a wake without flowers, and so dismally sad." But he had still refused to accept that there was anything unusual. "One dies and others take his place; don't they say *chinos* are like ants?" he had reflected that afternoon, but had later regretted saying as much to old Juan Chion.

"Besides, there's a peculiar smell in those places where lots of Chinese live. Don't you think, Juan? I don't know what it can be, it's a sweetish pong, like steam from a laundry. It seeps up your nose and you automatically think: that smells of lots of *chinos*. Isn't that right? The tenement has a long passage, with one door after another and a communal bath at the end, past a few sinks and metal water tanks. If it hadn't been for the *chinos* and their smell, it wouldn't have seemed like a *chinos'* house, but it's been that for over seventy years."

"What do we know about the guy?" Conde had asked Manolo, still feeling the eyes of those *chinos* silently drilling into his back.

"Pedro Cuang, seventy-three, born in Canton, emigrated to Cuba in 1928 at the age of thirteen. He only returned to China once, last year, but came back after a month. He was a dry-cleaner and received a monthly pension of ninety-two pesos. He lived alone, had never married and had no family. Just your average *chino*," the sergeant informed him, putting his notebook in his back trouser pocket in a gesture Conde knew was his and which his subordinate was shamelessly plagiarizing.

"And why the fuck would anyone want to kill an old man like him?" Conde had asked Manolo before entering the scene of the crime, as he greeted the policeman posted by the door.

"I swear to you, Juan, the smell of *chinos* multiplied by five and grabbed me by the face like the hand of fate intent on strangling me. But I went in. They told me nobody had touched anything … And I almost felt like crying, you know? You're lucky: you're married, you live with your daughter and own this house, but anyone who wanted to depict loneliness would be truly inspired by Pedro Cuang's room. A narrow bed, a dirty mattress and a sheet full of mends, and a piece of wood against the headboard, doubling as a pillow, I imagine. A piece of string in a corner where two or three shirts and some trousers were hanging. Two chairs with broken seats. A small kerosene stove and on the floor, by the bed, a tin full of water containing five very long pipes like the one you sometimes use. The dog was next to the bed. A mongrel with long white hair, it must have been half poodle, or half Maltese. The dog still had the rope around its neck that had been used to hang it … On the table by the stove were two plates, two small dishes, a few bottles and a box containing a set of dominoes. And the rest of the room was full of cardboard boxes: boxes of old magazines and newspapers, with cleaning cloths and tins and battered pans, boxes of soap, toilet paper and tins of food he must have kept for years. There was even a box of china plates. Like thirty boxes, mostly open, their contents emerging as if their entrails had been ripped out … The first thing I asked myself was, why did that man go home to China and then return to live in that stinking slum? Why, Juan? So many things littered the floor that nobody could tell whether anything was missing. I later asked and apparently nobody *does* know whether anything is missing. But your countrymen are the pits: you never know when they don't know or when they prefer not to know …"

Pedro Cuang had still been hanging from a ceiling beam; the end of his pale tongue, bitten by his teeth, stuck out. He was stark naked and there was a pool of shit, urine and blood on the floor. Conde had studied the corpse for a moment and thought *He's the skinniest chino I've ever seen.*

"And now comes something you're probably familiar with, Juan: they'd cut off Pedro's left index finger, and on his chest, using a razor blade or sharp knife, etched a circle with two arrows that made a cross, and in each square they'd cut smaller crosses, like multiplication signs ... you get me?"

"Look at this," Sergeant Manuel Palacios had added, showing him a nylon bag he'd picked up from the table by the stove. When the next-door neighbour, the one who had found him, had touched it, it had fallen from his right hand. There were two copper tokens, the size of a cent coin, that carried the same marks they'd cut on Pedro Cuang's chest. A circle with two crossed arrows and four smaller crosses.

"It st'lange, mighty st'lange," Juan Chion finally agreed, downing the last drop from the glass of rice wine he'd only brought out to accompany the meal.

"Hey, Juan, you've been living in Cuba for over fifty years, tell me just one thing: why don't you speak Spanish properly?"

Juan broadened his smile.

"Because I don't feel like speaking like yourr people, Mario Conde," he said, making an effort to round out his syllables and mark the *r* as if it was an exercise he found exhausting. He smiled and reached for the lieutenant's glass.

"Now you're being a sly old *chino*, right?"

"Somet'in of the sort ... Don't be stupid, Conde, the *r* doesn't exist in *chino*."

"Well, well ... So how do you say *roller coaster*? Or *trigger*? Or *generator* ...? Won't you pour me another drrrop of rrrice wine? Well, the fact is I spoke to the neighbour who found him and it was like speaking to a wall. He grinned or looked serious but could only manage '*Chino* not know, policeman, *chino* not know.' And all the others say 'not know' even more, but somebody must know something, must have heard something ... And your daughter is police and you certainly know I can't get to work without a fucking clue as to why they killed Pedro Cuang, cut that finger off and made that mark on his chest. Manolo says – I mean, the sergeant who works with me – that he's sure the man had money, but I doubt that: look how he lived. Although we didn't find a single cent in his room, and that's very strange too. But perhaps all the mess was just to put us on the wrong track or whatever ... Or do you think it was a case of revenge and that all the things they did to him make some kind of sense?"

Juan Chion nodded and, like a wise man, opted to fill Conde's glass to the brim.

"Thanks, my friend ... The other big news is that a month ago they found a consignment of cocaine in Chinatown, two blocks from where Pedro Cuang lived. Cubans were caught with the drugs, but the detectives suspect what they've confiscated isn't even half of what came in. And they got three kilos ... One of the men in prison says they stole a parcel of coke from his home ... As far as we know, that's never been found."

"And did Ped'lo have cocaine?" asked Juan, suddenly perking up.

"I don't know, but we found nothing in his place ... Although that way of killing him ... Look, my friend, this is my problem: I don't have a clue about what might have happened or what they did to the dead man, and I need your help … I don't know if you knew him, but he was a fellow countryman."

"Me be policeman?" drawled the old man, smiling, of course. "Juan Chion be policeman in Ba'llio Chino. No, Conde, me can't." And he underlined his feelings with a sustained shake of the head that threatened to become perpetual.

Mario Conde looked him in the eye and choked down the plea he was about to make. As Lieutenant Patricia had warned, if he couldn't find someone able to open Chinatown's secret doors and help him crack the business of the severed finger, the crossed circle on the dead man's chest and the two copper tokens bearing the same sign, there would be no way he could get to grips with that devious, defiant death he had to investigate. Because if he was convinced of anything at that moment, it was that nobody, at least in Havana's Chinatown, had bothered to mount that spectacle as a simple game of mirrors to put the police on the wrong track. Besides, he thought that Pedro Cuang's trip to China seemed too strange, and even more so his decision to return to his filthy bolthole in Havana where he'd lived for over forty years, storing tablets of soap, tins of Russian and Bulgarian food and old newspapers … But, to tell the truth, his biggest problem was that everything seemed extraordinary in the lives of those *chinos* who'd been living in the heart of the city for over a century and were still remote and different, about whom people barely knew two or three clichés that were useless at that point in time: fried rice, Chinese pomade for headaches, the dance of the lion and the existence of films without subtitles, like the one Conde had seen years ago in the Golden Eagle, surrounded by an applauding, chortling, weeping audience of Chinese who were ecstatically enjoying a spectacle he found incomprehensible. The clichés you summoned to feed the images of what the hell a damned *chino* was, alive or dead.

"Conde, business of *chinos* so'lted by *chinos*. Do you get me?"

"No."

"You silly, Conde."

"You're sillier. This isn't *chino* business ... You know only too well how all this works. Your daughter is police and she told me you could —"

"My daughter is Cuban and cannot speak for me."

Conde counted to ten. He needed a massive dose of *chino* patience if he was going to penetrate that tall story. "For fuck's sake, more clichés." He launched a fresh attack with a mix of guile and forcefulness.

"Juan, your daughter is Cuban and is police and you know what it means to be police. And it was your daughter who put me on this job and told me you could help me. And you *have* to. Because there's a dead man, and because people are dealing with cocaine in the Barrio Chino, there are illegal gambling dens, and, I hear, a clandestine rum and beer factory ... and as I am police, I at least have to find out who killed that wretch and why. Juan, nobody deserves to die like that. And I'm not going to solve this shit by myself. If you don't help me, the dead man stays dead and the guy who killed him lives splitting his sides with laughter and eating spring rolls in The Mandarin. Besides, Patricia told me you knew Pedro Cuang —"

"Only by sight."

"But I know he was a friend of friends of yours … Please. Juan … What if the murderer isn't a *chino*? Why are you so sure it's *chino* business?"

The old man sighed, shook his head again in that same negative, pendular movement, until he smiled and said: "Listen this, this wisdom from my count'ly: once there was a man who made a well at the side of a path, and all the people who passed by p'laised his deed, because was ve'ly good well for eve'ly one who lived a'lound there and needed water. But one day someone d'lowned in the well, and everybody c'liticized the man who built it … Do you get me?"

"Yes, and even I know the song about the *chino* who fell down the well … That's just one more tall Chinese story, Juan, very nice and very educational, but it's a story, and now what you must do is help me find a real-life killer … Nobody will criticize you for doing that."

"But, Conde —" he protested without much conviction, and the lieutenant seized the moment.

"I'll be here to pick you up at 8.30 tomorrow morning, Corporal Chion," said Conde, as he washed out his wine glass and bowed to Juan. Before he left, he checked the old man was still laughing and shaking his head of hair that was standing on end. "Just think about what I told you … Particularly the business of the finger and the cross on his chest, agreed? Help, for your mother's sake," he begged, straightening the revolver in his belt. "And tell Patricia to call me when she can," he added as he went out into the street, unable to imagine the hurricane of secrets and sorrows past and present that were now obsessing his model *china*.

Conde enjoyed the peaceful solitude he found in the street, but when he reached Calzada de Infanta, he found he'd just missed his bus. And it had driven away with some ten empty seats. As if to say, no, Conde, luck does not shine on the righteous.

3

Mario Conde had always loved books – and would always love them, and even more so when an unexpected turn in history led him to make a living by buying and selling old books as an alternative means of survival in a country where for years, in the midst of the most devastating crisis, people simply struggled to get through the day and reach the next morning alive. First as a reader, then as an aspiring writer, and in recent years as a bookseller, he had enjoyed books, sought them out and even dreamed about them as much as he did about baseball. And that was quite something.

"Do you really like reading a novel where everything's a lie as much as watching a baseball game where everything's for real?" his friend, Skinny Carlos, had once teased him.

"Novels don't just tell lies, and what you see in a baseball game isn't necessarily true," he'd replied, so as not to disturb the harmonious relationship between the two activities that was solidly established – in *his* mind, at any rate.

Despite his battered neurones being crammed with nostalgia, flashbacks and other detritus, there was a tidy, well-lit area set aside in his mind for the long-term storage of insights from books that had captivated him over the last twenty of his thirty-five years. This process deepened especially the moment he became a regular of Lame Calixto, the devoted librarian at Víbora Pre-Uni. Calixto was a survivor (with one less leg) of what had formerly been the high school, where, when Conde was a pupil, thanks to Calixto's advice and passion a splendid, airy library was created, conceived so a fifteen-year-old could find whatever a fifteen-year-old should. And after satisfying the curricular needs of a pupil set on digesting whole books and not the abridged versions his teachers gave him following instructions from the Ministry, Lame Calixto wisely and enigmatically fostered the boy's sentimental education, cannily adding authors and works to those he'd already ingested: Dumas, Salgari, Verne, Twain ... Calixto broadened Conde's horizons with the revelation of myths and heroes at the root of all psychological complexes when he entered the world of Greek and Latin classics; then he tried to get him to understand the hidden meanings of the journey into hell described by Dante and the search for earthly paradises in the chronicles of the conquest of America, and subsequently guided him thorough those nineteenth-century French and Russian novelists who challenged your patience (Conde later discovered that the librarian hated English novels of that period, especially Dickens, heaven knows why) and finally led him, via Hemingway, Fitzgerald, Dos Passos and Carson McCullers, to the edge of the river so that Conde duly graduated from pre-uni properly equipped and would now have to cross to penetrate more entangled jungles: Faulkner's world, say. Or Camus's. Or Kafka's. Or Salinger's forest of ambiguities with his crazy but so appealing characters. Or Raymond Chandler's urban fables of death and ethical concern, Vargas Llosa's daring narrative structures or Carpentier's carefully tied bundles of culture and subjunctives.

In all those long apprenticeship years that transmuted into a love of books and, finally, into an addiction capable of making him dream he would or could be a writer – that ended in the catastrophic move from this dream to a real attempt to write and be published in a school magazine that never got beyond issue zero – Conde continued to feel that same passionate love for baseball, the ball game that had always been much more than a game for Cubans: it stood for a way of life that lay deep in the marrow of the culture and consciousness of those islanders. An inalienable feature set in the bloodstream. His gallery of heroes housed a range of characters who coexisted in excellent neighbourly relationships: the Count of Monte Cristo, Seymour Glass, Fabricio del Dongo and baseball aces Pedro Chávez, Tony González and Raúl "Guagüita" López, the most mythical closer who ever graced Cuban baseball. Sequences from novels and hitting and pitching averages. The stories of characters and the chronicles of championships. Existentialists and industrialists. Tyrians, Trojans and baseball players. All mixed up.

"So you're a policeman who reads? How the hell did you get into that?" Major Rangel had enquired one day, soon after Conde joined Headquarters. "Or this?" he added, touching his uniform.

"One day, when I was sixteen, a lame librarian told me reading would allow me to see the world through the eyes of others."

"And what's that supposed to mean?" the major had asked, lighting up a cigar.

"One day this guy told me I was ready and gave me a book. He had wrapped it in newspaper so you couldn't see the real cover and said: read this, it's a book about slavery, but if you read it, you'll be freer. It was a novel that presumably nobody should read in Cuba … A dangerous book."

"And which book was that?"

"*Nineteen Eighty-Four*. And it changed my life. I've read it some ten times. And it really has made me freer. Because it showed me there are many ways to be a slave."

While he observed the black hulk of the building that had first housed the high school and then Víbora Pre-Uni, now converted into a technological college specializing in God knows what, he noticed that the windows of the wing once occupied by the library had no shutters, while the fence that had once protected the school space now lay on the ground. Conde felt the passage of time hadn't brought improvement; rather, it had smoothed the way for regression, and he was sure that would have woeful consequences for his country. He remembered the three years spent in that venerable place, where he had not only become a little bit freer thanks to literature, but also must have grown into a man at a dizzy speed in the periods they were dispatched to cut sugar cane, at a rate of ten hours a day or until they'd met their daily targets. The place where, fortunately, he'd joined a clan of friends, some of who remained pivotal to his life. He painfully reflected on how reality had reduced that period of grace and dreams to tatters and how the world where he now lived seemed increasingly less like the perfect world portrayed in the rhetoric and heat of the historical moment, and more like a world whose construction was still in progress, a world that brought precariousness and prohibitions and required sacrifice, rejection and even physical mutilation.

Conde dismissed those drab reminiscences that were so present in the building that echoed with the voices he could hear across the years, and slowly walked along the street that led to Skinny Carlos's house and also to the house where Karina lived – the last woman he had bedded, who had blown her sax and turned his life upside down, only to vanish like a dream, or like her music – (or at least she said that she lived there; who the hell could tell if she was lying or not?). Unhappily, the fate of once great pleasures seems to be to wither ...

He needed to speak to Carlos that night without any alcoholic baggage, because he'd had uneasy presentiments ever since he'd talked to Juan Chion about the violent death of his fellow countryman, Pedro Cuang. There'd been something ambiguous in their conversation and the old man's reactions, and Conde suspected much more was at stake in Chinatown (and especially in Patricia's father's mind) than a corpse that had been mysteriously branded. Which was why he had also needed to speak to Lieutenant Patricia, since he needed to warn her of his premonition and remind her that some doors were better left alone, and, naturally, should never be reopened.

Carlos was sitting in the doorway in his wheelchair, to which he'd been confined for the rest of his life. Nothing remained of his lean frame from their pre-uni days: pounds of flesh now drooped, like hanging pouches, from his arms, neck, chest and legs, as testimony to the frustration Conde also assumed was his. *Why him and not me?* No, Carlos didn't deserve the fate he had been consigned by a stray bullet that had found him – because he'd been required to make that sacrifice – in the midst of a remote and alien war.

"Hey, didn't you say you were up to your eyebrows in a case?" Carlos raised his hand for Conde to hit with his palm.

"Yes, they've messed up my vacation … but in exchange my house is the cleanest in the world and smells like — "

"You eaten?"

"Like a mandarin."

"And you drunk?"

"Just a drop."

"Would you like a swig of rum?"

Conde looked at his friend. His question was enough to undermine all his firm pledges on behalf of sobriety. How firm?

"Where's the bottle?" he asked, already ripe for combat.

"Half a bottle," Carlos explained, not wanting to raise too many hopes. "It's in my bedroom. You go and get it. And don't make any noise, the old girl's gone to bed."

"This early?"

"She says television is a load of shit, and she prefers to dream."

"A wise woman," agreed Conde, smiling sincerely.

In fact, Josefina's life had been reduced to looking after her son and tolerating the presence of that wild bunch whose friendship, thirst and hunger kept the invalid afloat. The old lady deserved her respite and escapism.

Carlos went on to confirm his friend's remark. "Do you know what she says now? She says she dreams she's cooking. That she prepares banquets for us and that whenever she needs an ingredient, she only has to hold out a hand to receive it ..."

"Well, she should invite us into her dreams one night."

With the help of two glasses of rum, and the night-time breeze blowing though the doorway, they talked until one in the morning. Conde spoke of his fears and premonitions and his desperate masturbating, driven by the traces left on his retina of Patricia's body and motored by that damned hypnotic, all-conquering female smell impregnating the atmosphere in his bathroom.

It was only when they were saying goodbye that Skinny, with his ability to touch the raw nerve ends of his friend's existence, revealed a piece of information that set off every one of Conde's red alarms.

"Oh, hell, you're almost off and I forgot ... Tamara called. She's just back from Italy. And she says she'd like to see you."

4

When Juan Chion first arrived in Cuba, he was eighteen
with a pair of strong arms and a single idea in his head:
he was going to earn lots of money and become rich in
that new world where the genuine item flowed like the
limpid water in his country's mythical streams. Then he
would return with his fortune to the hamlet in Canton
where his parents, brothers and sisters barely survived,
always freezing stiff and ravenous, sowing rice and poach-
ing fish from muddy, voracious rivers that were in no
way mythical and didn't belong to them, since even the
rivers in his country were owned by somebody. With the
money he earned on the other side of the world he'd
buy a plot of land for himself and his family and would
be famous and beloved, like a god descending from
the highest, snowiest peak: his single, almighty gesture
would thus change all their destinies. Juan had heard
about lots of *chinos* who had made their fortunes in the
Americas, and he, at eighteen, was sure he too would
join that happy band.

But Juan Chion, whose real name was Li Chion Tai,
was too honest a man and never earned enough money

to become rich or return to his hamlet: when it flooded, his parents drowned in that same river that fed them, two of his brothers died in a peasant rebellion and Li Chion Tai never did find out whether the rest of his family, who scattered across that vast and alien country in search of salvation, discovered what they were looking for ... From then on he lost contact with his relatives and became deeply saddened: that was why he left the job and friends he had in Havana and went to live in Cienfuegos, where he had a cousin who'd arrived on the island two years before him. Cousin Sebastián found him a job on a fellow countryman's ice-cream stall and Juan sensed he was recovering that nice feeling of being part of a family. But one fine day his cousin informed him that he was going to the United States. Despite the many obstacles to emigrating, his cousin had contacted a Greek captain who sailed in a boat under the Panamanian flag. For two hundred pesos that captain would take him to New Orleans. Juan, who had no money, had to stay in Cienfuegos, cherishing Sebastián's promise to send him the necessary dollars to join him in San Francisco, where everyone insisted it was easier to establish a business and get rich in a few years.

Sebastián and Juan, who were full of brotherly love for each other, hugged and hugged the morning when the cousin, alongside other countrymen, boarded the boat whose prow pointed towards a wealthy future. Juan waited months for a letter from Sebastián, but never heard from him again. Then he started to make enquiries via all the *chinos* who had relatives in San Francisco, or in any United States city, but nobody knew a Sebastián who also went by the name of Fu Chion Tang. It was only around 1940 that Juan finally discovered the fate of his last known living relative: all the Chinese who had embarked on that voyage had frozen to death in the boat's cold storage and, rather than go to the United States, the ship had sailed towards Central America and the captain had ordered the freezer compartments to be turned up to maximum. The frozen corpses of the thirty-two *chinos* had been thrown overboard like blocks of ice into the Gulf of Honduras, after being stripped of the money they had managed to hide and the few valuables they were carrying …

With no news from Sebastián, Juan had returned to Havana in 1936. Thanks to a friend he found a job in a grocery store and soon after met and fell in love with a jet-black woman with hard tits and an ass that was inconceivable in the Far East. Chinese Juan and black Micaela married in 1945 and a few years after, when they'd almost given up hope, life rewarded them and they became parents to a healthy, beautiful child. From then on, Juan worked up to sixteen hours a day behind the store's counter only so his daughter could live, not like a wealthy girl, but at least like a human being, and in the future could be an educated, cultured woman, with a fate different to that of her father and her family, whether on the black or *chino* side, worn down by servitude and centuries of slavery. That's why in 1958 Juan left the block where he lived with his wife and, with the help of the money he'd been saving to go and meet his cousin Sebastián or for that permanent dream of a return to China, he picked up his goods and chattels, crossed the frontiers of Chinatown and rented a house on Calla Maloja, the least violent part of the city centre, in a modest building with the luxury of two large windows that looked out over the street, the place where Patricia had lived from the age of two.

Mario Conde and Sergeant Manuel Palacios let old Juan Chion do the talking. They'd never heard him come out with such a flow, and hearing him tell his stories was a singular privilege granted them because the *chino* had finally embraced his new status as an auxiliary policeman. The old man didn't comment on why he had been dressed and ready for them when they reached his house, but Conde knew that Patricia (*Where has that woman got to? Why the hell doesn't she call me?*) must have influenced his decision. Chion would do anything for her. *He dotes on her*, thought the lieutenant as he resumed the thread of his story in the car driven by Manolo and heading to Chinatown.

That was where Juan Chion had first lived when he arrived in Cuba, like almost all Cantonese. His first job had been washing pots in the Golden Lion, the inn run by Li Pei, where maestro Cuang Cong Fen had taught him to prepare the most exquisite dishes for every palate in the world. Beef cooked in sweet and sour sauce, with mango pieces, sesame seeds and pineapple chunks, for example. But the Chinatown that Juan Chion's reminiscences were beginning to depict wasn't at all like the dirty, gloomy streets along which the three men now walked: all that was left of the physical splendour of those streets were their ancient names (Zanja, in honour of the aqueduct that first brought water to the city; Rayo, after the lightning that killed two blacks), the Chinese characters on the balcony of an occasional family business or cooperative, and a degree of indestructible grime. This Barrio Chino was dying; the one that Juan had known in 1930 was alive and kicking. You didn't make much money, but in its heart you had all the good and evil pleasures of life on hand – opium and mah-jong, theatres and whores, secret societies and the lottery, parties and fights, gangs and usurers, cheap taverns and restaurants with private rooms had romanced Juan Chion, and Conde thought that all that remained of the spirit of a place that the old man's words suggested was so colourful and lively was a whiff of its elusive, pungent aroma and the memories of a few *chinos* who were a dying breed and as old and ornery as Juan Chion or the late Pedro Cuang. It was obvious that they were crossing a sad, battered, shabby, moribund place in the centre of a city that shared its tragic destiny. Then, as so often, Conde felt an attack of nostalgia powered by an energy he'd never witnessed. *I would like to have seen that,* he thought. *But I'd never have wanted to experience it, least of all like these* chinos.

"So if there was so much going on, why did you go to live outside the area?" he asked the old man.

Juan had wanted Patricia to grow up in a house outside Chinatown, because at the end of the day it wasn't a good place to be if you wanted to make something of your life, and he had a dream for his daughter's future. The Barrio was like Canton but wasn't Canton, and the Chinese lived poorly. They were only interested in earning enough money to go back to China at some point, although in the end they never would. But it was obvious that to earn money, enough real money, you couldn't just work in a grocery store, a laundry or a fruit and vegetable

47

store; that was why gambling, drugs, prostitution, fraud and a horrific Chinese–Cuban mafia had mushroomed, and Juan wanted to be well away from all that ... Besides, after what had happened to Sebastián and since he had become a father, he no longer wanted to go anywhere.

"Me diffe'lent kind of *chino*, no?"

"So why?" asked Conde, trying to get the most he could from the old man's torrent of words, although he immediately grasped he'd got it all wrong.

"Because perhaps *chinos* have same eyes, but we not all same ... And that's enough for now, I not the killer," answered Juan Chion, and this time he didn't smile.

"All right, all right," the lieutenant conceded. "But just tell me one thing: did you find out the meaning of the circle with the two arrows? Now that you've mentioned it, it sounds like the Chinese mafia, right?"

Juan Chion shook his head energetically.

"No, it doesn't, that's why it so st'lange, Conde. You know, seems like the stamp of San Fan Con, the Chinese saint, the g'leat captain, 'light? But San Fan Con don't kill that way, he use sword and cut off head. Let's go see my f'liend F'lancisco, the man who know most about San Fan Con." His smile faded for a moment. "But don't torture him with police stuff ... F'lancisco is in ve'ly bad shape and mustn't be upset ... And, Conde, get this in head, *chinos* aren't little ants."

Mario Conde was trying to catch his breath and adapt to the all-enveloping darkness of the long staircase to the top floor where the Lung Con Cun Sol Society was based when he saw Juan Chion had reached the top and was giving a man a hug. Their Cantonese words were an enigmatic mumble, then Patricia's father introduced them in Spanish as colleagues of his daughter.

"Please to see you, F'lancisco Chiú," said the old man, and bowed to them in the style of Juan Chion.

In the semi-darkness Conde thought he caught a glimpse of Francisco laughing as well. He was very old, no doubt older than Juan Chion, and skinnier than the late Pedro Cuang, with a yellow tint to his skin that Conde thought originated from his liver rather than his ethnicity. He was clearly a very sick man.

"Pancho Pat'licita's godfather. From same hamlet in Canton, and we worked in same g'locer's store," added Juan Chion, who made another bow before raising his hand to Francisco's shoulder. "And me godfather of Panchito, Pancho's son. We *compad'les*, as you Cubans say …"

Conde and Manolo smiled dutifully and followed the old men into the Society's main room. Two long rows of empty, dusty wooden chairs with shabby wickerwork lined the sides of that sizeable space. Towards the back a small square table preserved the decisive finale to a game of dominoes that, judging by the layers of soot, must have finished several years ago. Francisco pointed to some armchairs and walked to a large window with shutters that were falling apart, and finally they had light. A sunbeam crossed the dust and abandon and fell on the centre of the room, and Conde and Manolo scrutinized that place that had stopped in time, as they could see from the *Selecciones del Reader's Digest* diary opened at 31 December 1960 between the luminous drawing of a peaceful lake at the foot of a snow-capped mountain, and an Alka-Seltzer clock that had also come to a halt at some remote hour. *So twenty years are nothing, as the tango goes, I guess? And thirty are on their way to being something?* Conde wondered as he contemplated that set from an English mystery film and noticed how his hands had been blackened by the dust of lost time: that society was as moribund as the district that had fostered it, to which *chinos* had ceased to come after the now historic year of 1949, when the great revolution that followed the great march led by the Great Leader had closed the frontiers of that large country with a barrier more solid and impenetrable than the Great Wall of imperial times.

In the meantime, Juan Chion and his fellow country-man had started talking in Cantonese again. It was a prolonged hum, reinforced by successive nods and a few broad, gentle hand gestures as all-encompassing as a con-juror's. More than once those hands and their Chinese shadows met in the air, touched, shook and then resumed their languorous dance, as if words weren't enough and they needed that cutaneous communication.

"You ever heard of San Fan Con, Conde?" Manolo whispered in his ear.

"I think so. When my grandfather said that somebody was more evil than San Fan Con, it was because they were really evil. But I don't know where the hell he got it from, because he didn't have a drop of Chinese blood in him."

"So he's an evil saint? Saintly and evil?"

"I guess so … You know these *chinos* …"

"No, I don't."

"Isn't the smell getting to you?"

"It smells Chinese, right?"

Conde nodded, accepting Manolo's verdict: of course, it was that vague but unmistakable smell they'd defined the previous afternoon as a *chino* smell. And he also noticed that the humid heat of May was absent from that anachronistic place: the unreal atmosphere created a coolness in the air, as if they were miles from the cauldron of the street they'd just walked down.

"Did anyone tell you in the end if Pedro Cuang had money or knew people who were dealing in coke?"

"No, Conde, nobody mentioned that or anything else. It's a bastard. I don't understand these *chinos*: the bastards act as if they don't understand me and I — Did you hear that?"

A noise reached them from the back of the Society, sounding like a piece of furniture being moved carefully, though it still squeaked slightly. Conde leaned to one side and saw a man's shadow on the wall walking towards a square of light and crossing it.

"Somebody's there, and I reckon he jumped out of a window," he informed the *chinos*, and wasn't sure how to act.

"Well, nobody there," smiled Francisco Chiú, adding, as he broadened his smile, "Oh, it was only a kitten ..."

Conde had no choice but to repay one smile with another: if he wanted his help, he couldn't afford an argument with Francisco Chiú over the size of that bipedal cat.

Juan Chion and Francisco stood up and Patricia's father addressed them: "Let's go see San Fan Con."

Conde thought, *No, I won't be shocked, even if I see San Fan Con in person*, and followed the old men.

Another darker, dustier staircase led to the Society's second floor. Francisco led the way, far too slowly. Juan Chion followed, and his firmer steps sent up a constant grey mist. Conde felt his eyes become irritated. He was dying to ask questions, but held back. When he returned to Headquarters, he'd go and have a word with Lieutenant Patricia and their boss, Major Rangel. *Why the hell does it always have to be me?* he was thinking as Manolo whispered in his ear: "There's a window and it looks over another terrace … That's where the cat jumped from."

Francisco opened a door at the top of the stairs and a faint light shone down. The door shut behind him and the pitch-black returned.

"Why all the mystery, Juan?" asked Conde, trying to see the expression on the old man's face. "What on earth does seeing San Fan Con mean?"

"You see now, you see now. Ve'ly f'lightened?"

"No, not in the least …" he said, looking for a cigarette in his shirt pocket, which he put between his lips before he heard the old man say:

"Don't light."

Conde smiled. He either smiled or ran out, he thought, when a stronger light shone. Francisco moved out of the doorway and Manolo and Conde followed Juan Chion into the Lung Con Cun Sol Society's holy of holies.

"Policeman never been here before," Francisco informed them and went off to open another window, adding: "I do this for goddaughter, Pat'licita …"

The light suddenly flooded in. *An altar?* was Conde's first thought. It looked like one, but it wasn't, although it had two parts, like a main altar and a smaller one for the purpose of worship. The piece that could be classed as the latter had been carved from dark wood and planed smooth with utmost care, first by a consummate artist and now by woodworm, ants and tropical humidity that had eaten away part of the lovely piece. Tall porcelain vases stood on either side; profusely decorated and gilt-edged, they contained bunches of dried flowers. Beyond them, bronze censers – he imagined for burning incense or aromatic herbs – rose up, with feet shaped like snakes' heads and crowned by rearing lion-dogs that bared their teeth and tried to look ferocious, although their effeminate faces rendered them pathetic. At the centre of the piece, supported by two plaited wooden columns and at the back of the section that might be the main altar, was an embroidered silk tapestry, framed by the wood's most elaborate arabesques: it represented the image of four fat mandarins with long moustaches and ponytails who were talking to each other, perhaps discussing the fate of an entire nation. The face of the mandarin in the centre, whom the perspective placed slightly to the fore, was a bright red, as if it had just emerged from an oven.

The two *chinos*, standing in front of the altar, bowed their heads three times as they did when greeting each other, and Juan took two pieces of wood from the shelf – ear-shaped and flat on one side, perhaps they were seeds – which he banged together several times while uttering a litany Conde decided was a prayer. Juan returned the pieces of wood to their place, and only then did Francisco enlighten them, pointing to the tapestry: "The one with long beard and b'light 'led face … is Cuang Con, or San Fan Con, as they call him in Cuba."

A circle with two arrows and four small crosses. A dead man and a dead dog. Two copper tokens similarly inscribed. A severed finger. And now the mythological hero, Cuang Con. *How am I going to disentangle this Chinese puzzle?* wondered Conde, as he watched Manolo's intrigued expression. His colleague was looking at the embroidered cloth and Francisco's mouth while his head moved from side to side like – what else? – a Chinese fan, going from the informant with the absurdly yellow complexion to the legendary mandarins embroidered on a background lit by the splendours of a dawning sun.

The tapestry represented four captains who had become sworn brothers as a result of their military campaigns: Cuang Con, Lao Pei, Chui Chi Lon and Chui Fei. They were the princes who during the Han dynasty had founded the Great Lung Con Cun Sol Brotherhood so that forever and ever all their children, those blessed with the illustrious surnames of Lao, Cuang, Chion and Chui would be mutually protected by the divine guardianship of those fighting gods. In China and even in Havana.

The four titans were discussing the future of the kingdom. Their enemy had kidnapped the wives of the chief and older brother, Lao Pei, thus robbing their country of its fertility and future. Without women there is no beauty, there is no world, because there isn't even life, and Cuang Con, the most intrepid of the brothers, prepares to go to their rescue. He confronts and overcomes a thousand labours, he rides over meadows and mountains with his arm supporting a lance that weighs six hundred pounds and which only he can handle, and his cunning and courage defeat the rival armies; and one spring afternoon he returns with the kidnapped wives and restores hope to the country of Lao Pei. His immortal feat is inscribed in history and the hero becomes a god, and every year his descendants, before an altar like that, pay eternal homage to the man who saved their future.

"But he wasn't a saint, was he?" asked Conde, scratching his arms to dampen his longing for a smoke. "I mean, he wasn't sanctified like the Catholic saints ... Why is he San Fan Con?"

Francisco's going to laugh, the policeman thought when he finished his question.

The *chino* smiled. "That happened here. He came here as Cuang Con, a g'leat captain, a mythological he'lo, but was Cubanized into San Fan Con, and as he bright red and a saint, you know, captain, blacks say he Changó," said Francisco, still laughing, and Conde reflected again that despite the ascension performed by Francisco (which put him at the level of the great Cuang Con), he could still beat an honourable retreat: he understood less by the minute and felt ever more stupid and uncultured while at the same time suspecting that some of those laughs were mocking his innocence, credulity and ignorance. Because it had turned out that Cuang Con wasn't just San Fan Con, but Changó, the blessed Santa Barbara, with his red cloak and sword in hand ... *It's all too much,* he thought.

Meanwhile, still smiling, Francisco had taken from the mantelpiece that looked like a small altar a bamboo cane cut like a long glass. It contained some very thin rods, also made of bamboo, inscribed at the end in Indian ink with a number and some letters, which he now clattered together like maracas for concrete music. Francisco explained that Cuang Con was Lord Luck: each rod indicated a path in life, and the one that bore a circle with a cross made by two arrows was the worst path possible: the way to hell, where traitors, murderers and adulterous women went. Some people in Cuba said that was San Fan Con's most negative sign, that a man so marked could expect every unhappiness in both worlds: of the living and the dead. As he heard that explanation, Conde felt painfully heartened: at last he understood something and, at the same time, his hunch was strengthened that the marks on Pedro Cuang's body didn't relate to a mere game of appearances; at the very least they indicated a path that led to that dark, dusty room belonging to the Society. Or at least it passed through that way.

"Me don't believe that, captain, but there people who do. It's my count'lymen making black witchc'laft and blacks making magic with *chino* things. You get it? Ped'lo Cuang owed and someone collected, and that's why he got sign of San Fan Con."

"So he was killed by another *chino*? In revenge? And did they cut his finger off because he had informed on someone?"

"Oh, captain, me not know," said Francisco, still shaking the bamboo cane. "Now you want to know your path?"

Conde didn't have time to think of a way to put pressure on Francisco before seeing a rod emerge from inside the cane Francisco was still shaking, just one, that seemed to float over its companions as if a hidden magnet had separated it from the rest and brought it to the policeman. The top of the rod, like all the rest, carried symbols and a few letters. Might his destiny be contained there?

"No, thanks, I'd rather not know …" said Conde, driven by the power of his superstition as he pushed the rod back into the glass. "But I'd like to look at the one with the cross."

Francisco stopped shaking the container and moved over to the light from the window. He looked at the rods and selected one, which he handed to the lieutenant. Followed by Manolo, Conde also stood in the light.

"It's similar, but not the same," noted the sergeant, while he sketched the incomprehensible symbol in his notebook.

"Francisco, what Pedro had on his chest also had little crosses here, in those four squares … Isn't there another rod?"

"No, captain, not one with four c'losses … It's st'lange, 'light, Juan?"

"Francisco …" Conde hesitated to say it, but did so. "Would it be too much to ask you to lend me that rod? I promise I'll return it. I need to take a photograph of that sign and —"

"No, that belongs to San Fan Con and —"

"A man has died, Francisco," said Conde, trying to make his voice sound as solemn as possible.

Francisco seemed to think as much as his brain was capable of, and then took a decision.

"All 'light, all 'light," the old man conceded. "But you must b'ling it back or you'll suffer curse of San Fan Con …"

"I swear by my mother I'll return it," Conde declared, already imagining the impact of a possible Chinese curse.

"I don't see any *chinos*, but I can smell them," Conde muttered, and felt pleased with himself. His sense of smell had deteriorated years ago when he started smoking, which was why he wanted to know what pungent qualities that peculiar smell contained for him to be able to distinguish it from among all the smells of a city rich in scents and, above all, in stench. The long passageway in the tenement on Salud and Manrique had fallen silent. On the clothes line two T-shirts as full of holes as soldiers fallen in the cruellest war were battling against the wind and, by the jamb of the third door, an old man was reading a cutting from a Chinese newspaper.

"Look, there he is," Manolo said when he saw Pedro Cuang's next-door neighbour.

"What his name?" asked Juan Chion.

"Armando Li," the sergeant remembered, greeting the old fellow by that name. "How are you?"

Armando read for a few seconds more, then looked up. He considered smiling but decided against it. He stared at the newcomers, and his eyes lingered on Juan Chion's face.

"Good day," he said finally, and got up with a nimbleness that belied his apparent age.

"So, Armando, this is Juan Chion. He's a relative of mine. He came to explain to me, you know …"

Armando nodded, said, "Me know nothing," and then produced a smile.

Conde gazed at the old man's greenish teeth and thought how he despaired before a smile that could encompass four thousand years of culture. He raised an arm, about to threaten the old man, but Juan Chion seemed to guess his intentions and jumped in first. He said something in Cantonese and Armando, after concealing his smile again, replied and the two old men disappeared into a room.

"Well, that's us sorted, isn't it?"

"Didn't you want Juan to help you? That's just what he's doing. The *chinos* who don't want to sort things in our presence."

"Know what, Manolo? We're only beginning and I've already had a bellyful of *chinos* and San Fan Con …"

"Well, watch that stomach, because this is turning ugly … Because if that sign isn't San Fan Con's, then what the fuck is it?"

"It's smelling Chinese again, but tasty Chinese this time, right?" Conde asked, though Manolo knew that that final inflection was simply a rhetorical move. He merely wanted agreement, not a reply, and the sergeant half-heartedly went along with him.

"Yes, but what's he putting in?"

"Don't you worry, whatever it is it will taste great. That's my experience."

"And this wine isn't half good, right? On the sour side, but it slips down a treat."

"Too true," said Conde, taking a sip of the ginger wine Juan Chion had offered them.

In the kitchen the old man was now singing a mournful Cantonese ballad that seemingly complemented his culinary inspiration and helped him process his ideas.

When he'd finished his conversation with Armando Li and they'd gone out into the street, he'd asked them for time to think, and Conde's questions had only prompted invitations to lunch. It was obvious that something had happened that morning that had improved Juan Chion's state of mind.

"Hey, Juan!" – Conde projected his voice from the sitting room – "so did Pedro Cuang belong to the San Fan Con Society?"

"Of course, of course," the old man replied before resuming the lyrics of his Cantonese song.

"And what do you think that sign they drew on his chest means?"

"Something bad, 'light?"

"Doesn't the severed finger sound to you like the *chino* mafia?"

"You see too much films, Conde. No *chino* mafia in Ba'llio. Only heap of old *chinos* and shitty Cuban c'liminals …"

"So why did they kill the dog? Don't you usually say they bury dogs alive with their masters so they can guide them through the other world?"

"Sometimes do, stuff of legends," said Juan Chion only after sustaining a falsetto on a long line.

"Hey, are you *chinos* always so complicated?"

The reply didn't come immediately. It came when Juan Chion peered out of the kitchen.

"*Chinos chinos*, Conde … Food's 'leady." He smiled and beckoned to them.

Conde and Manolo walked over to the table which the old man had already set. Although they weren't slow to ask what was in the dish he was offering them, the *chino*, holding a beautiful soup tureen decorated with blue and feathered serpents, asked them to be patient and said he hoped they enjoyed a good meal.

Juan Chion placed the tureen in the centre of the table and sat down. Not waiting a second, Conde stood up and peered into the mysterious concoction: yellow and dark green strips floating in a thick, whitish broth that had the consistency of jelly.

"Hey, it smells good," allowed the lieutenant, though he hesitated before tucking in. "Now please tell me what it's got in it."

"*Chino* dog soup," said Juan Chion, unsmiling, and Conde and Manolo's faces immediately expressed their inevitable disgust.

"*Chino* dog? What —" began Conde, when the old man recovered his smile.

"Naw, Conde, me playing … Teasing, as you say. Look, it's soup made from 'lice and white fish, with eggs and st'lips of cabbage. T'ly it, t'ly it."

"And what else did you put in?" persisted Conde while the *chino* served them.

"Basil and mint, that why it smell so good, 'light?"

Conde inspected his plate and glanced at Manolo's ever disconcerted expression. "I'm going for it," he thought, and made the leap: he put his spoon in the steaming jelly, blew on it a couple of times and finally tried it before Manolo's expectant gaze and Juan Chion's steady smile.

"Hey, guys, it tastes really good," he said, sticking his spoon back into the viscous ancestral dish.

Juan Chion watched them eat contentedly, and suddenly came out with: "I thought something."

"Right you are," gulped Conde and prepared to listen to the result of the old man's long ruminations.

Juan Chion thought lots. When he went to Canton, Pedro Cuang had commented that if things went well, he would stay in China, but he returned after a month and never said why, although he did tell people in the Barrio that the China he found wasn't the China he'd imagined. However, many people thought the dead man had returned because he must have had money in Cuba: for years he'd worked as a bet collector for a clandestine bank that dealt in illegal gambling in the Barrio, and as the Chinese loved to lay bets, the collectors must have earned a tidy sum. Although not only *chinos* bet: apparently, all the Barrio was at it, including little boys and girls, as they say.

The police had dismantled the bank precisely when Pedro was in China and he had emerged unscathed because it suited nobody to say that an old man who was absent at the time was the guy who collected the loot and lists from all the other bet collectors. *Chinos* weren't informers, and that business could only become public knowledge now the old man was beyond the reach of human justice … As far as people knew, Pedro Cuang wasn't involved in drug trafficking or in other murky waters, and certainly had never betrayed or informed on anyone. But Juan Chion believed that there is always somebody ready to kill a *chino* who might have money, perhaps a lot of money, and that's why it wasn't at all odd that not a single cent was found in the dead man's room. Pedro must have had money. And he also thought that there was a code that is inviolable in the eyes of his fellow countrymen: deception and betrayal are paid for with death, and though nobody could be sure, perhaps Pedro Cuang, despite being Chinese, had betrayed or informed on somebody.

"Make your life easy now, Conde?" concluded Juan Chion, and it was Conde's turn to smile.

"You've given it to me on a plate, haven't you? Now all I need to know is what the hell I've got on that plate: deception, betrayal, an illegal gambling bank that no longer exists and a *chino* who we don't know if he was involved in the drug trafficking everybody's talking about or if he really had money, or just ought to have had ... A *chino* who was strung up with a cross on his chest that now turns out not even to be the sign of San Fan Con, a saint who at the same time is and isn't a saint, a mafia that no longer exists, but if it did, it wouldn't forgive a betrayal, a *chino* who doesn't betray but probably does ... Piece of cake."

"Oh, Conde, Conde," the old man lamented. "The snake got tail and got head. 'Leach tail from head and head from tail. G'lab snake. You always 'leach the other end. But take care ... if you g'lab head, snake bite."

"A snake?"

Luang-me Wu had lost the last of his children, but showed no sign of grief. He organized a fine funeral, received condolences, and friends even saw him smile. Time passed, and Wu tilled his land again, looked after his animals and drank a few drops of liquor after he finished:

he continued to behave as he always had, and didn't even respect the usual mourning period. When he noticed this, a neighbour who had thought Wu to be a wise and honest man reproached him for his lack of feeling. Then Luang-me Wu told him: "There was a time when I lived without children and I wasn't depressed. When my last child died, I returned to my previous state. Why must I be sad?"

Juan Chion inhaled smoke from his pipe and stayed silent for a long time so Conde and Manolo could consider the tale, before telling them that this story was one of the most famous in the Taoist tradition. And although he knew that things functioned differently in the real world, and that dead loved ones should be mourned, the story attributed to Luang-me Wu really did impart truths Conde and his colleague should learn: for example that everything, animal and human, enters the world with its own path, its own *tao*, but at the same time perhaps nothing exists that can be eternally unchangeable. Everything becomes its opposite, the quest for happiness can lead to misfortune and even death, and the wise man must find the essential nature of things and always observe the natural laws of life, the *tao* marking out each individual's path in order to possess knowledge and come to know the truth. Because man's soul comprises the smallest particles of matter, called *tsin tsi*, that come into being and depend on the clean or filthy state of the organ for thought, the *tsin*.

The pipe returned to the table and Juan Chion smiled: "Clean *tsin*, Conde, clean it well."

5

As usual, he went into a state of ecstasy contemplating the house. Because of what he saw on the outside and what was on the inside, it was always the perfect house, the one that awakened most of his dreams and desires and would continue to do so throughout his life: even the momentary dream of remarrying, despite two previous experiences of matrimony that weren't exactly pleasant to recall.

The line of concrete sculptures opposite the picture windows on the ground floor seemed closely related to Picasso and Wifredo Lam, and were a distinctive feature of the building. But the huge panes of glass, the long windows with wooden shutters, the breaks in the straight lines of the structures and that patio with its beautifully kept English garden rounded off the place's visible delights. Hidden treasures included the library Dr Valdemira had curated over a long diplomatic career, with a select bibliography assembled from more than half the world, a room whose walls were graced with originals by some of the great names of the Cuban avant-garde, friends of the lawyer. But the greatest delight of the house was the one that, after Conde had come out of his trance of architectural ecstasy and bibliographic reminiscences, came and opened the door.

"Mario, how great to see you!" she said, stepping forward to kiss him on the cheek as the policeman put the brakes on all his impulses.

"Skinny said you were back. How did it go?"

Five months ago, at the beginning of that same year, 1989, Mario Conde had returned to that house and the life of Tamara, the girl he'd first fallen in love with, painfully so, when they had met almost two decades previously at Víbora Pre-University. But those visits, so satisfying in some respects, were tainted from the start by trauma: the trauma of the disappearance and later revelations about the death and shady dealings of Rafael Morín, the man who with his irresistible charms had stolen Tamara's love from Conde, even going on to marry her and father her child. The macabre circumstances which had put Conde in charge of the hunt for Morín, and the things he had begun to find out about that apparently straight-as-a-die eternal leader's manipulation, scheming, deceptions, corruption and multiple back-stabbings, had led, wonderfully and strangely, to Conde and Tamara making love in that very house and Conde reaching the highest possible level of ecstasy: the fulfilling of a desire he had harboured for almost twenty years.

The avalanche of dreams the policeman cherished at the time, which was so dramatic he even imagined taking the solemn step and promising "till death do us part", was suddenly halted by Tamara's decision to spend a while in Milan, where Aymara, her twin sister, lived, married to an Italian who, according to all the gossip, was filthy rich and a normal, nice individual. "So the guy can't be Italian, right?" Rabbit, the friend of Conde most addicted to logic, had quipped.

Tamara's departure had left Conde disarmed, even disillusioned, and it had been in that state of psychological, hormonal defencelessness that he had fallen into the orbit of Karina, a perverse, red-headed nymph with the gift of disappearing when Conde most needed her. In all that time and the subsequent weeks he had hoped Tamara would return, fearing she never would, as had been the case with so many friends over the years. But she had returned, had summoned him, and a jubilant Conde was now observing the earth-shifting movement of her buttocks (that magnificent ass, the size of which had frustrated the young girl's aspirations to become a ballet dancer) as she walked in front of him on the way to the patio.

Tamara left to percolate coffee while Conde analysed her reactions. After crossing the frontier they had violated several months ago, they'd reached deadlock, Conde reckoned, and it was up to her to end it: one way or another. The fact that she'd welcomed him with only a friendly peck on the cheek didn't augur particularly well. So why did she want to see him? Just to make him suffer at the sight of those hazel eyes that were always moist, and the crushing sugar-cane movements of her wondrous backside that drove, was driving and would drive Conde crazy?

They drank coffee and brought themselves up to speed on the generalities that courtesy required: the family's well, Italy, what can I say, fantastic … Venice, Florence, Naples, Rome, Siena, Bologna …

"I thought you probably wouldn't come back … With so many sights to see and after everything that happened …"

"Aymara wanted me to stay," she replied, almost glancing away from Conde. "I've left my son there, at least until the summer. I want him to forget everything it's possible to forget …"

"So why did you come back now?"

This time Tamara did look him in the eye.

"I need to put some order into my life, and I can only do that here."

"Is there such a thing as an orderly life? I thought —"

"Don't start, Mario. You know I don't like that irony of yours."

"Sorry. But you're planning something I can't imagine ever happening. I'm that stupid …"

She rewarded him with a smile and Conde didn't think twice: he hurled himself over the precipice.

"And do I appear anywhere in that reordering?"

Tamara smiled again, but immediately resumed the grave tone she'd adopted at the start of the conversation.

"I'll be frank: right now I don't know. I'm still too mixed up, and rushing into anything might be dangerous for us both. Rafael fucked me up a lot, and I don't want more scars. Besides, you're …"

Conde was nonplussed by that sentence that hung in mid-air.

"A policeman?"

"You're very complicated …" she said finally.

"In what way?"

"In every way, including the worst: you fall in love ... and that influences a relationship. And obviously I wouldn't want you to be hurt by any rushed decision ..."

Conde lit another cigarette and gazed at the lawn he'd first stepped on twenty years ago, the day when twins Aymara and Tamara had held their fifteenth birthday party, accompanied by music played by the one and only Los Gnomos, the most in-demand, legendary band in La Víbora at the time. He decided he was in such poor shape that a romp with Tamara, which might bring fresh bruises, wasn't going to change his physical or mental state all that much. Providing there was a romp, of course. No, he'd never understand women: either they were all perverse or mad or deliberately made things difficult in the worst possible way (sometimes without falling in love). As far as he was concerned, things were astonishingly simple: first we romp, then we think. However, as he knew only too well, implacable Tamara was in charge, and in his desperate state his only option was to trot out his ironic gentleman's repartee.

"Fine. Don't feel hassled. Tomorrow morning will do ..."

Tamara just had to smile.

"You don't have any choice."

"No. And it's not going to get any better ... So why did you want to see me?"

"Just to see you. So you'd know I'm around ... Isn't that enough?"

"That's almost too much. It's a real honour you bestowed on me," he reacted, unable to restrain himself yet again. She drove him crazy to the point of foolhardiness.

"Know what?" Tamara asked after an uncomfortable silence. "In Italy I met a friend of my brother-in-law, a Spaniard, and I won't deny that I liked him and he liked me …" Conde felt that sucker punch and gasped. "Then I started to think about what my life might be like with him, living in Barcelona, entering his world and that of his friends, stories, people, memories that had nothing in common with my stories or memories … and I couldn't see myself there. I know my life isn't going to be easy here. First there was Dad's death; then all the business over Rafael … I'll now have to depend on my work, and things are very much on the brink in Cuba. What's happening in the Soviet Union and all that area is no joking matter: I think they've opened a door they'll never be able to shut. They're throwing shit at the fan and the fallout will splatter even here. These may be difficult times for everyone. But I feel I belong here: to this country, I mean. It's my life, more than anything else. You know how a life is many, many things, not just a house like this or a job or status and privileges … it's also the things that make you who you are and not someone else. And the person I am, I am here, not in Milan or Barcelona …"

"But your sister —"

"We are twins, we're a lot alike, but we aren't the same person. Aymara has a different lifestyle. Different to the one I know … She says I'm the family fool. And I expect she's right."

Conde dared. He stretched out his right hand and grabbed Tamara's left.

"I'm sorry if I said something idiotic … I'm very happy you've come back. But the truth is, I missed you far too much … Take whatever time you need to think, really … I don't know how, but I'll be waiting for you. It's my speciality: I spend my life thinking, although what I think rarely resolves anything, and I've been waiting for twenty years," he said, standing up. "Now I'd better go, I've urgent business to see to … My work, you know … I'm looking for somebody who killed a *chino*."

Tamara came back to earth with a bump and reacted with astonishment.

"A *chino* has been killed?"

"Yes, though you might find it hard to believe, *chinos* do get targeted … And when it happens, they even die. Even though they've been practising t'ai chi for a hundred years …"

"If you say so," she replied, smiling.

"I'll drop by soon, but call me whenever," he said, ending the conversation by leaning in towards Tamara and planting a kiss on her cheek. A kiss from a desperate friend investigating the death of a *chino*.

One of Mario Conde's most recurrent fantasies was that a bar existed in Havana where they knew his favourite tipple. Conde could walk into that bar – naturally somewhere cool and shadowy, with clean glasses and tumblers, like a bar ought to be – at any hour of the day or night and, once he'd perched on a stool and leaned his elbows on a corner of the bar – which was made of dark, elegant, highly polished wood – the barman would come over, and after a brief, almost familiar exchange of greetings, he would pour his drink, without Conde having to place an order. In that ideal place (with ceiling fans and high stools and an old freezer with multiple doors), a place that man's soul was clamouring for at that precise moment, they knew Conde preferred three-year-old rum, made in the old Bacardí distillery in Santiago de Cuba, which he liked to drink in a tall glass, with a few drops of lemon juice and a small ice cube. ("The usual", the barman would say, as he served him.) All very simple and formal, but at the same time natural: like the rum he drank. Of course, in that bar they also knew that when Conde was drinking alone, it was because he wanted to *think*, not because he was a fucked-up lonely alcoholic in the middle of a romantic crisis or something else, an animal racked by despair.

But, like so many other dreams, it was impossible to translate that simple bar to the hostile, worn-down objective reality of the city where he'd been born and had lived ever since and where he'd continue to live in the new century, as he pondered on his police incursion into Chinatown, and, to make matters worse, was still searching for solutions to his relationship with Tamara and for that bar where they would serve him his tipple automatically.

However, what really riled the policeman to the point of fury in 1989 was that generally, even when he had to order his drink, it was never the same bar, let alone the same barman, because everything on that island had to flow dialectically from negation to negation, perhaps seeking absolute nothingness via that route, nor was it possible ever to find the same drink in each bar: there wasn't ice, or lemon, or they hadn't received rum from Santiago for months, and – the final straw for the detective lieutenant – that day they had no rum, or any other intoxicating liquor.

After a long day of Chinese revelations and the beginning of a long period of waiting, that night Mario Conde needed, like never before (that's a turn of phrase: no need to exaggerate, less so when rum was at issue), that bar to exist, his very own, so he could cleanse his *tsin*, with swig after swig of pure alcohol, of the infinite impurities he must have accumulated after a long stretch of inappropriate activity. He suddenly thought how his *tsin* was like the dirty head of a video recorder that requires a good clean, *necessarily* using alcohol, to once again emit pristine images and sounds. And although the concept of disinfecting his *tsin* was a new idea, the certainty that rum allowed him to do almost everything he wanted in life – to briefly escape his daily tedium, to feel free of inhibitions and guilt, to let his consciousness fly to a state where oblivion was possible and time ceased to exist – was by now a tried-and-tested habit he liked to abuse with welcome frequency.

"There's no bar and no rum, but I'll clean my *tsin*, even if it's with petrol … Not water, because that's corrosive …"

Three closed bars, two where they only sold cigarettes, and markets where the rum – even a choice of brands – was closeted behind the high, still totally prohibitive barrier of the dollar bill, led Conde to a dive in La Víbora where Jacinto the Magician, a retired industrial chemist, strove to distil alcohol from the most unlikely ingredients. Conde (always concealing his police affiliations) had to knock on two doors, pass three wrought-iron grilles and invoke the name of his friend Red Candito, the alchemist's partner, for Jacinto the Magician to take him to his well-stocked shelves in a small zinc and wood room in his backyard.

"Hey, kid, what tickles your fancy?" asked the Magician while he poked a finger up his nose hunting for seemingly elusive snot.

"I've a choice?" asked an astonished Conde, breathing a sigh of relief at the thought of likely liquor.

"I've got Fire Ball at thirty pesos, Coffee Cream at fifteen, and Drop Your Panties at twenty-five ... Oh, and passion-fruit wine at eight a bottle."

Conde felt a stabbing pain in his liver and dismay in his saliva glands but, despite those objections from his organs, he decided to jump down the well of despair.

"What's the chemical make-up of your concoctions?"

"That's easy: Coffee Cream is basic alcohol filtered through coal and grey paper, to get rid of the bright colour. Frankly, I don't recommend it, it's for people who've lost it already" – he made a gesture to indicate a screw missing – "but Fire Ball is something else: I distil that, using sugarcane and grapes and a drop of good alcohol, and bread when I can't get yeast. All very healthy ... Ecological, as they say nowadays. Say, have you ever drunk *orujo*?"

"*Orujo*? What the hell is that?"

"A grape-based liquor they make in Spain."

"And have *you* ever drunk *orujo*?"

"Never ... Where am I going to find *orujo*, son? But I'm not a chemist for nothing, right? That's why I imagine it's rather similar ..."

"I love your power of imagination. But tell me more about what's on offer …"

The Magician looked at Conde, pondered, moved his finger in another attempt to capture that snot, then opted to continue his spiel.

"Well, Fire Ball is, I suspect, more or less like *orujo*, and that's why it's more expensive … and I make Drop your Panties from spuds and yeast, and it's red-hot. Drink a bottle of that and you can do anything: from robbing a bank to streetwalking. It's what most people buy, you can guess why —"

"I don't like the sound of it … I've got nobody's panties to strip off … hey, why don't you remove that snot, wash your hand and give me two bottles of Fire Ball?"

With his supplies under his arm Conde headed towards Skinny Carlos's, but on the way he decided to summon Red Candito as well and, from a public phone, called a neighbour's house he used to leave him messages. Luckily, Candito was home.

"Red, I've got two loaded rifles tucked under my arm," he announced when his friend came on the line.

"So what else do you need?"

"I'm on my way to Carlos's."

"But what else do you need?"

Conde smiled. "Are you reading my thoughts?"

"I'm reading fuck all, Conde, I just know you …"

"All right, I thought you could lend a hand with San Fan Con … As you're the tribal theologian."

"Don't be an idiot, Conde. But I'm on my way …"

The Brazilian soap had begun and, from the sidewalk, Conde listened to the drama of those characters whose lives with their happy endings brought relief to the bitter day-to-day toil of Skinny Carlos's mother as she bore the physical and spiritual cross of her son's disabilities. Not allowing old Josefina to get up or miss any of her television drama, Conde kissed her on the forehead, stroked her hair and left her glued to a screen that emitted its signals in black and white. Though he remembered that at some point they would need a serious conversation about the gastronomic dreams the old lady had recently been experiencing: if she dreamed like she cooked, just listening to her would be one big party.

Asking for no permission or authorization he walked through the kitchen, and while wolfing down a plate of boiled potatoes garnished with tuna and onion slices, he picked up three glasses in which he put ice and, still chewing on his last mouthful, he went into the room where his friend was looking out of the window and listening to music on his headphones. He must be listening to Creedence, reckoned Conde … Or perhaps Chicago? Without announcing his presence, he opened one of the litre bottles and poured generous slugs of Fire Ball into two of the glasses. He smelled his and immediately felt his respiratory tracts clearing, scorched by the fifty-degree-proof liquor. So this was *orujo*? Like fuck it was. He held his breath and tried it: as usual, the first sip was bad, but this one was the worst yet. A ball of fire rolled down his larynx, and as it descended must have singed Mario Conde's *tsin*, and the *tsin tsi* fled like enemies of the people transformed into panic-stricken rats in a popular film from the People's Republic of China.

"Hell!" he snorted and then tried the alcohol again,

which this time went down with less fuss, though with the same intent.

He took the other glass to Carlos, who was still absorbed in his music. It was terrible to see him always in his wheelchair, looking through the window at the trees in the yard. *What on earth can he be thinking about?* wondered Conde, gazing at the profile of his old friend, whose anatomy overflowed the arms of the chair he'd been sentenced to for life. Conde surreptitiously placed the demon glass between his friend's eyes and the infinite. Without saying a word, Skinny smiled, took the glass and gulped down half its contents.

"Red-hot lava, Conde, what the fuck is it?" He started in his wheelchair and tried to tear off his headphones with a swipe.

"The Italians call it *Fulgore di Treno*, the Spanish *orujo* and the *chinos* – you know what they're like – *Tsin-cleansing Elixir* … What do you reckon?"

Carlos took another swig and nodded.

"It'll get us smashed, but better than nothing, right? Is it a product of the Magician's distillery?"

"Right first time," said Conde, draining his glass. "I bought two litres because I need to think a bit and then obliterate everything. In that order."

"If you bought this, it's because you want to forget even your name …"

"If only."

"What's up, wild man?"

"I dropped by Tamara's."

The subject was of interest to Carlos, who finally removed his headphones.

"And?"

"It's too complicated, Skinny. Our Tamara is turning into a philosopher and Red Cross nurse. I'll tell you, when I'm smashed —"

"Don't be such a pansy, Conde, don't leave me dangling …"

"You just dangle in there. What I want to talk to you and Candito about is the damned mess I've got into, and which another woman is to blame for … Just imagine, I've got a dead *chino* linked to a gambling bank, probably to drugs as well, and most likely witchcraft or Chinese mafia stuff, because they cut a finger off and drew a circle and a cross on his chest …"

"Sounds tasty," Carlos admitted, after downing another swig.

"Sounds shitty," said a voice behind their backs, and they turned round to see the mulatto Candito walk in; he shook their hands and settled himself down on a corner of Carlos's bed. "So where did this happen?"

"In the Barrio Chino."

Candito grabbed the glass that was waiting for him, poured himself a good swig of Fire Ball and downed a gulp. The mulatto's reddish head savoured it, as if he were savouring a great vintage wine, and gave his informed verdict.

"Hell, the Magician is improving."

"Was it worse before?" asked Skinny, as if he thought that was impossible. He took another swig.

"It's drinkable, right?" Red Candito took another sip and concluded: "It's like *orujo*."

Conde and Carlos exchanged glances. Something was

very, very bad in the kingdom of Denmark if Candito associated that shit with a remote beverage known as *orujo*. But Conde decided not to blur the conversation – at least at that early stage, on the first bottle – and waved at Carlos to dampen his curiosity.

"You see, Skinny? I told you … *Orujo*," he said, and chinked his glass against his invalid friend's.

Candito smiled slyly and got straight to the point: "So what's this Chinese tall story all about, Conde?"

6

"What's wrong?"

The sun shone rudely at 9 a.m., threatening to usher in one hell of a day. A sullen glow rose above the nearby bay and Conde, protected by his dark glasses, felt the shafts of light like burning needles on his eyes. He tried to smile at Candito but couldn't.

"You look greenish, Conde."

"And what colour do you want me to look, Candito? I've a hangover that makes me want to die …"

"You can't handle it like you used to, bro … hey, I woke up bright as anything and I drank the same as you."

"Come on, the ferry's here," said Candito, leading him by the arm like a blind man.

The old ferry that crossed the bay from Avenida del Puerto to the town of Regla had started to dock and Conde thought it was a bad idea to go sailing with such a chronic hangover. It was a short trip and the sea seemed calm, but he might empty out his guts at the surge from the smallest of waves. Nonetheless, he took a deep breath and boarded.

The previous night, when at Candito's request he'd drawn a picture of the signs etched on Pedro Cuang's chest, Candito had told him to forget San Fan Con and all that Chinese gibberish, since he was on the wrong track or they'd put him on the wrong track: Red was convinced the arrows, circle and four crosses was a sign of Palo Mayombe, witchcraft from the Congo, and that they had cut off the finger to be used in a *nganga*, a cauldron which took the place of an altar. But if they wanted to be sure what the signs meant and find out about *ngangas* and *palo* symbols, Conde would have to visit Marcial Varona, the wisest, most respected *ngangulero* among all the santeria priests living in Regla, the mecca of Cuban voodoo.

Looking at a distant spot beyond the whitewashed walls of La Virgen de Regla, the policeman managed to complete the short crossing without the threatened vomit materializing, but when he stepped back on land he suddenly felt nauseous, as if his drunkenness was reactivating.

"You've gone really pale, you idiot," Candito warned him.

"Let me get some fresh air, it'll pass," Conde answered. He took a painkiller from his shirt pocket and chomped on it, absorbing all its bitterness. Then he lit a cigarette and gazed at the sea. He felt the bilious juices settling down, and spat on the ground. "I swear I'll never ever drink another drop of rotgut."

Candito laughed and forced Conde to laugh with him.

"You must be kidding, Mario Conde, you've been saying that ever since I've known you."

The parish priest walked by dressed for a service, or perhaps on his way back from administering the last rites.

"Know what? I swear by that priest's mother."

*

"Zarabanda," declared Marcial, putting his cigar back in his mouth.

That black could be one, two hundred years old, or whatever. Covered by a white woollen cloth, his head contrasted starkly with his jet-black skin, marked by every possible wrinkle and concertinaed into stiff folds. But it was the old man's eyes that caught Conde's attention: his eyeballs were almost as black as his skin and bore an expression that in the past, when Marcial was young and strong, must have been terrifying. According to Candito, Marcial was the grandson of African slaves and had lived his whole life in Regla, where he had been initiated into the religious secrets of the *palo* sect and become a *mayombero*. If that wasn't enough, he also acted as a *babalao* in the Regla de Ocha and many people judged him to be the person who knew most about Yoruba santeria. And if that still wasn't enough, Marcial was also a member of the ancient *abakuá* cult of the Makaró-Efots, one of the oldest cells of that secret society that had come from Calabar in slave ships, and, for many years, had occupied the highest position among the luminaries of that fraternity. But when Conde spotted a certificate from the Great Consistory of Grade 33 of the Cuban Masons granted to brother Marcial Varona on a wall next to a Catholic altar watched over by a crucifix and the Virgen de Regla, a black-faced Cuban saint, he realized he had found the man he needed: a bottomless source of knowledge and a living example of what it meant to be Cuban. Candito had forewarned him that talking to the old man was like consulting an old tribal guru, the man able to mentally hoard all the tribe's stories and traditions, something Conde would very soon confirm.

The effects of the sea breeze that blew underneath the ceiba tree Marcial had planted in his courtyard seventy years ago gradually re-energized Conde's whole being, and he felt the excellent coffee served by one of the old man's great-great-great-granddaughters awakening his intoxicated neurons one by one.

"Zarabanda is *nganga* from Congo worship, but also belong to Lucumi Oggún, or Yoruba santeria, as they say nowadays. Oggún is the master of the forest and metals, and is also St Peter, the one who hold the keys to heaven, you see? That's why Zarabanda isn't a genuine *palo* but a Creole mix, you understand me?"

"No," Conde admitted with all the sincerity he could muster, feeling unable to appeal to his sense of irony, and asked his macerated brain to make a manly effort to absorb all that totally cryptic, academic information for an individual who, of his own volition, had ended his relationship with all religions on the same day when, compelled by his mother, he had taken his first and last communion.

"You see, my son ... *Palo monte* is the religion of the blacks from the Congo and *nganga* is the seat of the mystery of that religion. The Ark of the Jews, the chalice ... *Nganga* mean spirit from the other world. A dead man is trapped in the *nganga*, physically gathered in the iron cauldron, where various attributes are placed so he can be the slave of a living man and do whatever that living man order. *Nganga* is power and is almost always wielded to do evil, to put an end to enemies, because *nganga* fuse all supernatural forces from the cemetery, where the deceased reside, and the powers from the *monte* – forest – where the sacred *palos* – sticks – from the trees reside, which is where the spirits live … And that's why the religion is called *palo monte* …"

"So what's all this got to do with *ngangas*?" Conde asked, showing him the doodles again, since he'd given up trying to understand and was now simply trying to shift the conversation from the abstractions of an intangible world to the material squiggles on a dead *chino*'s chest.

"That is a Zarabanda signature, the sign that's always written at the bottom of the iron cauldron that receive the *nganga*. That sign is the seat of the strength, as *the power* is called, and is the basis of everything else the cauldron contains. Take a good look at the drawing: the round part is the earth and the two crossed arrows are the winds. The other crosses mark the axes of the world, always four in number … No need to search any more, what you see there means Zarabanda … But the odd thing about that signature is it's a form rarely used today … Those who believe they know add more arrows and little flourishes, as if they mattered. What you see is the old signature, from the days when Cuba was a colony, the way my grandparents did it, genuine Congolese who'd come from there."

Marcial pointed to a precise spot, beyond the frontiers of the small town of Regla, over the sea. The beginning of everything.

"And is it true they put human bones in the *nganga*?"

"Of course. If not, how are you going to possess the dead? The *nganga* carries a thousand things, whether pure Congo or Creole mix with Yoruba santeria, like Zarabanda. But it must always have a man's bones, and best of all the head, the *kiyumba*, which is where bad thoughts, madness, hatred and ambition reside. Then it has sticks from the mountain, but not any old *palos*: sacred sticks, with *the power*; also thunderstones that have already tasted blood, animal bones, best from the fiercest animals, a little earth from a cemetery and quicksilver as it is never, never still. Oh, and holy water if you want it to do good. If not, it's not baptized and stay Jewish, that mean un-Christian – nothing to do with the religion of the Jews ... But if it is Zarabanda's *nganga*, as he own all iron metals, there is a chain around the cauldron, and you must place inside a key, a horseshoe, a magnet, a hammer and over all that Oggún's machete ... All those attributes are given rooster and goat blood to drink, and then it's decorated with feathers of many colours."

Conde felt he was losing himself in a world that went back along a path to beyond Mount Sinai, to the origins of human understanding. He had been brought before a mixture of cultures – and Marcial Varona was its living, exemplary representative – that he had always coexisted with, and even formed part of, though he was infinitely removed from its arcane practices. Those religions that had first been stigmatized by Catholic and Christian slave owners who believed them to be heretic and barbarous, then by the bourgeois who deemed them to be things done by dirty, black savages, and in more recent times sidelined by dialectical materialists who described them according to scientific and political criteria as remnants of a past that atheism has to overcome, embodied, in Mario

Conde's view, the charm of the human spirit's resistance and its will in defying the dictates of fate. The mysteries of that universe brought from Africa by hundreds of thousands of slaves had taken root on the island, had survived every social, economic and political onslaught and entered the flesh of day-to-day life: *paleros*, santeros, *abakuás* and *babalaos* (who were Catholics and Masons as well as practising those rites, were everything all at once) walked the same streets as him, under the same sun, drank the same kinds of rum, but were protected by a useful, pragmatic faith the policeman didn't have, the essence of which – its greatest benefits, secrets and substances – he felt were beyond his understanding. Is the Congo Zarabanda the same as the Yoruba Oggún, master of the hills and the trees, and the same as Christian St Peter, apostle on earth, rock of Christ's church and owner of the keys to heaven? If it didn't have water from a Catholic church, blessed by a priest in a surplice, was it a Jewish *nganga*? The revelation of the existence of that mixture of complementary and hostile religions, the multiple after-effects of the previous night's horrific binge, and the image of a *chino* strung up in a Havana tenement, his chest marked with an almost forgotten Zarabanda signature, combined in his aching head to suddenly produce an idea capable of giving him the shakes, like a small snake suddenly poking out its head (*or might it be its tail?*).

"So, Marcial … must the *nganga*'s owner know the dead man he puts in the cauldron?"

The old man sucked on his cigar twice and smiled.

"That rarely happen nowadays, because people use any dead man … They go to the cemetery and open the grave that's easiest to open or buy the bones straight from gravediggers … But it is much better if you know the deceased, because you can choose the most suitable corpse. Back in Africa, when there was a war, they carried off the most courageous or nastiest enemy's *kiyumba* … You know, if you want to make a Jewish *nganga*, to do evil, you must search for a deceased person who was really evil … because the spirit is still as evil as when it was alive on earth. And is sometimes worse … That's why the best bones come from the mad, and even better than the bones of the mad are the bones of *chinos*, the most rabid, vengeful folk on the planet … I inherited mine from my father and it contains a *chino*'s *kiyumba*, one who was in such a rage he committed suicide because he didn't want to be a slave … and you don't want to know the things I've done with that *nganga* … and may God forgive me."

A *chino*'s *kiyumba*, thought Conde's *kiyumba*, is difficult to get your hands on. But a *chino*'s finger is easier. The grisly yellow, emaciated image of Francisco Chiú flashed through his mind when he shook Cuang Con's wild cane of fortune and the way he spoke about *chinos* who practise black voodoo.

"Marcial, can a *palo monte* cauldron help revive its owner's health?"

"It can do anything, my son. Anything."

Mario Conde would always remember that in all his years as a police detective, he had managed to learn several things. He had learned, for example, that the most difficult cases usually had the most commonplace solutions and also that slow, routine police work is usually more efficient than hunches or prejudices, although he detested routines and scientific work and preferred to be guided by flashes of insight that were usually reflected in a pain in his chest. He had also learned that being a policeman was a dirty business that had fallout: dealing with murderers and thieves, fraudsters and rapists on a daily basis ended up giving you a distorted vision of life, and the smell of shit stuck to your hands and was immune to the best detergents: that was why he was almost never shocked when a policeman was corrupted and accepted backhanders, practised bribery or protected criminals ready to pay whatever the asking price was. And he learned, by dint of practice, that walking alone tends to be the best way to think, especially if you are a policeman addicted to premonitions and prejudices (Conde's were always prejudices), and not to routine.

The bitter taste of the last painkiller was still lingering but he now relished the feeling of his neurons settling down, even believing he was in a fit state to think. He said goodbye to Candito on the ferryboat quay and took the road that led from the port area to Barrio Chino, which he entered via the Calle Zanja shortcut. The large dark clouds filling the May sky and the steam opening Conde's pores were all signs that a torrential downpour was about to hit the city. But now he felt he was starting to move along clear paths, with something tangible to cling to, and that was why he'd called Headquarters and asked Manolo to computer search the history of that betting bank which had been broken up the previous year, while he assigned himself the no less arduous task of walking, thinking, learning, and even knowing, if that were possible.

From the moment old Marcial Varona had confirmed the Congolese origins and Cuban transmutation of the strange sign etched on Pedro Cuang's chest, and the possibility that the severed finger had been destined for a Jewish *nganga* (because it was a *chino*'s bone), Conde had felt he'd been heading into a cul-de-sac, and now he was sure that the ostentatious wrapping hid a much less sophisticated product. Killing an informer, if that's what Pedro had been, didn't require such an elaborate scenario, nor did it seem necessary to have enacted such a macabre performance if the aim had been to steal money that the whole district was talking about but nobody had seen. All that staging had begun to seem much less meaningful even if it had been related to some peculiar religious rite: there were *chino* bones in the cemetery, and you could get those without having to string up a hapless old man and his mongrel and create obscure paraphernalia that, as it turned out, wasn't so obscure if you asked the right person. In other words, the motives for Pedro Cuang's murder had been much more banal and material, and Conde was increasingly certain that the stuff about Zarabanda and his *nganga* was only a smokescreen, or useful diversion from what had actually happened. Could it be connected to the drugs that were hidden somewhere in the district? Or had the old man perhaps possessed a secret that related to the banker he worked for as a bet collector? Or had it just been about money? Nonetheless, he couldn't get the idea out of his head that the bone of an acquaintance had somehow ended up at the bottom of a *nganga* intended to cure a terminally ill man. But would Francisco Chiú have had the muscle to fabricate all those theatrics, including hoisting the corpse into place? Or, if he *was* involved in the crime, might he have relied on help from someone else? And how would Juan react if he discovered his friend was behind the murder? Better not even think about that ... The policeman just had to think, think and think, for Christ's sake!

Conde discovered that at that time, around midday, the baking-hot streets of the Barrio were emptying out. The surviving elderly *chinos* fled the muggy heat, and in their absence the doorways where they sat in the morning or at twilight didn't seem the same. Once again he was shocked by how little he knew about those men who had grown old among sordid, stinking streets where one of the most populated Chinatowns in the whole of Western society had once been sparkling and vibrant, and he felt sorry for the brutal uprooting those wretched people had suffered. They had crossed the seas escaping poverty and hunger, authoritarian governments and compulsory military conscription, and in the end had encountered things as horrendous as those which had led them to flee in the first place: contempt, lack of understanding, neglect and even agonizing forms of death, like the fate which had met Sebastián, Juan's cousin, frozen in a ship's hold. But most painful of all was the merciless uprooting that the economic success of a few had been unable to mitigate. The only salvation for those Chinese had been to create a ghetto and respond to contempt with silence, to scorn with smiles, to shouting with closed doors, and to surround themselves with a philosophy that seemed peaceful and at the very least helped them to tolerate life. And were they as vengeful and frenzied as Marcial Varona had claimed? *Perhaps*, he told himself, recalling Tamara's qualms and understanding why she had felt the need to return to the fold to find herself ...

Conde wondered how often the police had failed to solve those mysterious mysteries (he decided to let that repetition stand) that *chinos* could provoke with the hermetic habits they had developed as a form of self-defence. He was just starting to justify his own probable failure when he saw a boy selling mangos on the corner of Calle Salud and felt the need to eat one. Not out of hunger or desire: just pure necessity. He chose a mango that looked tempting. He gave it a rub to clean it a little and, leaning forward, sunk his teeth in, feeling his life melt into the taste and texture of the fruit. With his hands dripping juice and his lips sweetened by the yellow flesh that stirred up nostalgia for his happy mango-stealing childhood, he returned to the visible, aggressive reality of the tenement on Salud and Manrique. He walked back down the passageway and scrutinized the anodyne entrance to the nasty little room where Pedro Cuang had lived and died. Without a doubt, Francisco could have visited the *chino* without anyone thinking it strange or even registering his presence. Conde opened the door with the key he'd decided to keep. He didn't switch on the light, but slumped onto one of the chairs with a smashed seat, part of the murdered man's meagre inheritance, and felt gripped by a biting, familiar sensation: in the end, loneliness wasn't an Asian invention. He too had gone to bed many a night with a premonition that he wouldn't see another dawn, and his lonely, neglected body had spent many hours in that bed that was too broad for his melancholy. The loneliness of Pedro Cuang, killed together with his dog, seemed a special metaphor for his own abandonment: everything he saw in that room betrayed the slovenly mess solitude engenders. The sad inheritance bequeathed by a poverty-stricken life … And that was when he spotted it: on the table by the stove, well corked, still shiny and pristine, barely hidden by a bundle of old magazines. His hunch was too strong to have got it wrong, and he wondered why he'd not noticed it on his previous visit. He got up, used a chipped knife to lever out the cork and then took a whiff: it was rum, of course. At the end of the day there are things a man with enough experience will never get wrong.

Conde took less than a second to calculate the possible consequences of his action, and immediately persuaded himself that what he was about to do was the best antidote for a hangover, which was why he was doing it. He remembered that drunkard's saying – "hair of the dog" – and took a long swig from the mouth of the bottle, enough to clean out the mango taste, warm his throat, relax his stomach and even risk polishing a piece of his stained *tsin*. "Thanks, o deceased," came his toast and, before swigging any more, he spilt a drop on the floor. "For San Fan Con," he whispered, though he must also have invoked Changó, Zarabanda, Oggún and St Peter the apostle, all mixed up in the same pot that was … Jewish.

Bottle in hand, he returned to the chair and lit a cigarette. His third gulp was steadier and consigned any sense of guilt to the abyss. *What the fuck, who the hell knows where this litre willed to nobody would have ended up otherwise? ...* Thanks to the rum, the Chinese smell began to be an aroma you could live with ... He thought of his friend – *if Candito could see me now* – and smiled, then suddenly felt even up to joining the Long March. *Why were you killed, you old chino? Was that your tao? Is that why you came back from China? So you could die in this stinking den and provide a finger for a high priest's* nganga? he wondered, contemplating the beam from which the old fellow had been hung, and suddenly felt something in his head explode and the bottle of rum slide from his hands. He wasn't even conscious enough to feel his own body following the bottle on to that filthy floor.

When Conde finally reopened his eyes, he saw the beam again, but from a different perspective. He didn't know where he was or what exactly had happened, but his first reaction was a typical policeman's: he slipped his hand under his body and gave a sigh of relief to find his pistol was still there between his belt and his skin. The boom from a clap of thunder confirmed that the buzz in his ears was due to the downpour that had just been unleashed. Then he plucked up his courage and dared touch his head a few inches above the back of his neck, and found the sore spot caused by the blow, though he was reassured to note that his fingers were still dry. He hated the feel of his own blood. Then he remembered the cure Grandfather Conde had always applied when he was left with a big bump after receiving a blow to the head: he would wrap a peso coin in cartridge paper soaked in salt and vinegar and rub the bump, which would slowly disappear. The best part of his grandfather's remedy came when the cure was complete and he could lick the paper, which had that peculiar taste of salt and pure alcohol. He reflected that perhaps that habit was the beginning of his later fondness for the bottle.

He made a fresh mental effort and realized he was lying on Pedro Cuang's bed, with his head resting on the wooden pillow. Whoever had struck him had bothered to put him on the bed and hadn't thought to steal his pistol, which would certainly have fetched a good price on the black market. Conde concluded they hadn't wanted to kill or rob him ... He looked around and spotted the bottle of rum next to the bed, the contents of which had almost all spilled on the ground except for a small drop left in its belly. Without sitting up, he stretched out a hand, recovered the bottle, raised his head and emptied the dregs of the rum into his mouth. Though the stench from the bed was all over him, Conde decided to stay there a few more minutes, staring at the ceiling beams and waiting for his head, which had taken such a battering (both inside and out) over the last twenty-four hours, to regain a degree of stability. He wanted to think about what had happened, but felt unable to do so while he enjoyed the peace that unexpectedly suffused his spirit, cradling and rocking him as his *tsin* floated at will, clean and scented, rising like an ethereal vapour towards the ceiling until, overcome by sleep, his eyelids drooped and closed. Before he fell asleep, he remembered that he was there because he needed to solve the murder of a man for whom nobody in the whole civilized West or Far East had shed a single tear. And what if they had killed him as well? *How lonely are the dead*, was his final thought before dozing off.

When Mario Conde returned to the land of the living barely twenty minutes later, his headache had gone and he was unable to recall whether what was floating in his mind was the memory of something he'd once read or something he had just dreamed: he had seen a man in a bloodstained Chinese tunic pursuing a naked girl who wore long jade earrings. For his part, he was running after them and trying to take a photograph with an empty camera, just as another man, also in Chinese dress, hit him on the back of the neck. His hazy mind decided it wasn't a dream: that story of Chinese garb was from something he had read – Chandler, perhaps? He didn't have the answer. However, he was certain he'd been woken up by a hunch that was about to become a certainty, one that made him leap off the bed: a piece of paper was poking its yellow nose from beneath one of the ceiling beams.

"You back?" asked an astonished Juan Chion, who forgot to bow or even to smile. "What's up, are you ill? You b'light yellow …"

"Well, I like changing colour several times a day …"

Conde walked into the house, grabbed the old man's hand and almost dragged him into the dining room.

"Sit down there, Corporal Chion," he ordered, and sat down in the adjacent chair. "Read this."

The old man took the piece of paper Conde was offering him. The yellow surface of the paper was covered by two lines of pale, imprecise Chinese characters. The old man looked at it, then held it away from himself, trying to find the right position so he could read them better. Conde devoured a cigarette while he waited.

"It st'lange."

"You said that at least ten times yesterday. What the hell does it *say*?"

"Li Mei Tang. That someone's name."

"Is that all?"

"Conde, Conde. Li Mei Tang, third left, sixth 'light, t'lee."

"Really?"

"'Leally."

"So what does all that mean, my friend?"

"Me *chino*, not o'lacle."

Conde squeezed out the last drops of his intellect.

"They're directions, right?"

"Conde, you police, not me."

"It sounds like directions … but directions to fucking where?"

Juan shrugged his shoulders.

"It's written in Chinese because it was written by a *chino* …" Conde continued.

"T'lue."

"… so another *chino* could read it."

Juan Chion smiled and pointed a finger at Conde.

"See, *chino* ain't ants. *Chino* cunning bastards and myste'lious too."

"Too mysterious … And look what they just did to me so I wouldn't get to the bottom of any of their mysteries."

Conde turned his head and showed him the marks from the blow to the back of his neck.

"What that all about, Conde?"

"I think they whacked me so I wouldn't find this scrap of paper. The guy who hit me also went to Pedro's house looking for it. He wasn't interested in anything else … But he really hit me hard, it hurts like hell. Do you have a cure?"

"*Chino* pomade good for eve'lything."

"Well, smear some on, because I need to go and find whoever did this to me. It has to be the same person who killed Pedro Cuang … and I'm sure he killed him because he wanted to extract from him what was written on this scrap of paper. Pedro's severed finger was collateral damage …"

"Colla what?"

7

Major Rangel scrutinized Mario Conde, while puffing on the longest of Havana cigars as he sat behind his desk, enveloped in a cloud of bluish smoke. The lieutenant felt like his boss had inserted him between two glass slides and was studying him through a microscope lens as if he were a mutating virus.

"You look as if you've come straight from a dumpster," was the first, would-be scientific conclusion reached by the chief of Criminal Investigations Headquarters. "At least you smell as if you've been inside one."

"That's a *chino* smell, boss."

"A *chino* smell?" Rangel removed the cigar from his mouth and delicately tapped the ash into a Murano crystal ashtray, a recent gift from his elder daughter, who was married to an Austrian ecologist who roamed the world saving whales and Bengal tigers – though on a budget that enabled them to stop off in Venice and buy expensive glassware. As one does.

"I slept in a *chino*'s bed … But I'd better not tell you about that, man."

"I should think not. But do tell me how it's going,

because I've got things I need to pass on to you. I didn't call you here because I couldn't live without seeing you … What the hell were you doing in bed with a *chino*?"

"Halt right there, boss … Clarification needed."

Conde acted extremely respectfully towards his superior. Nonetheless, he felt at ease working with him and liked to tease him with his ironic repartee. Conversely, Major Rangel, who was so cutting with the rest of his subordinates, admitted – only to himself – that he had a weak spot for that irreverent detective who could be overfamiliar and even dared call him "man" and drop by his house so the major's wife would invite him in for a cup of coffee. At the end of the day, Rangel thought, someone has to put up with him; despite his obsessions and wayward thinking, that lieutenant was his troubleshooter. And every now and then he had to get his own back.

While he was explaining to Rangel that sleeping in a *chino*'s bed wasn't the same as sleeping with a *chino*, and telling him everything that had happened since Patricia had turned up on his doorstep, Conde sensed his ideas were finally coming together and moving him towards a discovery that would help him solve his Chinese case. At the same time, he was also a hundred per cent sure there were other invisible but even thornier issues around the murder. Sure, a dark shadow from the past hung over the *chino*'s death, and the removal of that darkness, whatever its nature, might have painful consequences. But he didn't tell Rangel about these worries that were still too vague, or that he still harboured a suspicion, however flimsy, that pointed to Francisco Chiú.

"So you're not sure that the dead *chino* is at all connected to the cocaine being shifted in the Barrio?" asked Rangel, dropping his cigar on the ashtray.

"Not at this point. Why do you ask me, man? Everybody keeps bringing up the business of the cocaine in the Barrio …"

Rangel leaned back in his chair and closed his eyes for a second.

"What I'm about to tell you is confidential. If anyone finds out I told you, they'll slice me down the middle. Get that?"

"Get it like the coffee you didn't offer me today …"

"Get that?" The major's tone of voice changed as he repeated the same question, and Conde perfectly understood the meaning of his fresh tone.

"Yes, I get it."

The cigar had gone out, but Rangel picked it up and held it between his fingers.

"There's a big investigation in progress into the cocaine circulating in Cuba. It's massive. There are loads of people working on it. If the drugs being trafficked in the Barrio aren't related to your murder, then forget it."

"But Major —"

"No buts, Conde. You just do what I say, for once in your damned life! Find out who killed the dead *chino* and go back on leave. And forget all about this conversation."

Although he didn't understand, Conde assumed Major Rangel's instruction must be driven by very concrete motives, and he had no choice but to respect his order.

"And what if the murder and the drugs are connected?"

"Well, you just stop what you're doing and come to see me as quick as you can before doing anything else. Get it?"

"Yes, I get it, I told you, like the coffee I never got."

"Right, so clear off," Rangel blasted, using his cigar as a cue to point Conde to the exit. "But you've been warned. Get up and go."

Conde stood up, straightened his shirt and began his retreat. But by the door he risked one last salvo: "Hey, man, you're stressed out … You should give your *tsin* a clean …"

"Get out, for fuck's sake! And go and take a bath!"

Conde crossed the office's reception area and headed out into the corridor. He took the lift and went to his tiny office, where Manolo was waiting.

"What did the major want?" enquired the sergeant.

"Nothing really: to offer me a coffee and talk about Confucius a while … You know how sociable he is."

"No, I don't," said Manolo, totally sincerely.

"So, what have you got for me?"

"Look," said Manolo, opening the folder that was lying on the desk. "March last year a policeman routinely asked a suspicious guy on Zanja and Lealtad to identify himself. The fellow got all agitated and, after seeing his ID card, the policeman asked him what was in the pouch he was carrying, and he ran off. They soon caught him: he was carrying several lists of bets for a bank that gambled on the Venezuelan lottery that you can pick up on short-wave radio. There was a round-up and three bankers were caught, but they only found the money for that day … Then things went awry: the boss of the business, one Amancio Valdés, had a heart attack and died three days after being imprisoned. That's when the other two bankers reckoned heaven was on their side: they said Amancio was the boss and looked after the money. In the end, they held the trial and the bankers got two years for illicit gambling and the bet collector got fourteen months, but not a cent more was ever discovered. Once those bankers were out of circulation, others took their place, and the lottery is still going big time in the Barrio. That's what I've got on the case, apart from the things you might be imagining by now: Pedro Cuang went to China when all the trouble started and returned when Amancio Valdés died. Too much of a coincidence, don't you reckon?"

"And those in prison are still in prison?"

"Positive."

"And did any of their families go on a shopping spree?"

"Negative."

"And was there anything drug-related in those shenanigans?"

"Two joints of marijuana that —"

"Just as well …" Conde sighed. "And what else did you find on Amancio Valdés?"

"More positive stuff: until 1959 he ran a gambling den in the Barrio and his cover was a laundry. And wouldn't it be a big coincidence if Pedro Cuang had worked there?"

"And was that the case?" Conde asked, quickly warning him, "If you say 'positive', I'll chuck you out of that window."

Manolo smiled and closed the folder.

"You're getting overexcited … Well, naturally, he worked there thirty years, until he retired in 1968. But the best is still to come," he announced, and began a pause he prolonged as he felt his boss's tension rising. "The forensic says Pedro Cuang had a stroke before they strung him up. Apparently they hadn't planned to kill him, but when he went all paralytic they must have taken fright and thought it was best to shut him up for good."

"Obviously they weren't planning to kill him or cut off his finger ... The old fellow was the key to finding Amancio's money ... So what else do we know about Pedro Cuang?"

"Next to nothing. As far as we know, he didn't have children, wasn't married and had no relatives in Cuba."

"But there was someone he could leave a message for."

"What message might that be, Conde?"

Mario Conde looked at the street out of the only window in his cubbyhole and saw the transparent spectre of heat rising and spreading after the rain. He regretted the dreadful state his mind was in, subdued by alcohol, knocks, Rangel's orders, *ngangas* and contradictory input: he couldn't think fast enough. But the fact that he could remove Francisco Chiú from place of honour on his list of suspects came as a relief to his lethargic brain. Then he decided to throw himself into the only promising opening he had. He took the paper with the Chinese characters out of his pocket and handed it to his colleague.

"This message ... The path to Pedro's – or Amancio's – money is inscribed on this scrap of paper ... Manolo, I'll buy you a meal if you can tell me the meaning of Li Mei Tang-third-left-sixth-right-tree."

The sergeant looked up from the paper and its Chinese ideograms and stared at his boss. When his eyes settled on a distant spot, his left eye seemed to become detached and try to hide behind his nostril.

"Don't go all one-eyed and tell me, come on!"

"They're directions, right? To a place where there's a tree, where there's a path that goes left and then another that goes right and something connected to somebody by the name of Li Mei Tang."

While he listened to him, Conde felt a light beginning to illuminate his mind and started to smile.

"Fuck, kid, now ain't you a genius?"

Manolo also smiled as he waited to see where the lieutenant's joke was heading.

"Don't piss around, Conde."

"Sure, I'll piss around, *compadre*. Come on, let's get the car and pick up Juan. The infamous Li Mei Tang must be buried in the Chinese cemetery. I bet you anything that's what it is."

"Now, now, right now? … Hey, what about my pigs, my friend, hey, what about my pigs, my pigs."

Manolo tried to reason with the repetitious, loud-mouthed guard but he insisted: no, no, no, it was cemetery closing time and nobody could come in to do anything, unless he had orders from the administrator. Besides, he had to go and collect the slops from a dining hall where they kept them back for him so he could feed his pigs (I've got five, five, he repeated) and he wasn't going to stymie that for the police, a dead *chino* or anyone. His pigs came first … second and third …

Making the most of the gravedigger's strident rant, Lieutenant Mario Conde and old Juan Chion acted as if they'd not heard and carried on down the central alley through the cemetery and counted three paths, turned left and walked between the graves, dodging the puddles left by the downpour. And on the sixth path, when they turned right, they found their reward under an ancient weeping willow: LI MEI TANG (1892–1956), engraved in gold letters on a red granite plaque. Li Mei Tang's tomb showed he'd been a powerful man in his lifetime, but the deceased didn't seem to have been left a flower for many years. The lid of the sepulchre had been stained by soil and resin from the trees, and the bronze rings for handling the slab had inscribed it with their green spirit.

"It's the stark truth, isn't it, Juan? We are so alone when we're dead."

The old man looked at him.

"Not all dead, Conde. You bet Li Mei Tang had company, 'light?"

"Did you know that the grave of a *chino* is a bad place to keep something? People believe you bury your dead with jewels and money, but, worst of all, the *babalaos* say that Chinese bones are the best for making 'Jewish' cauldrons."

"What me always say, *chinos* useful for eve'lything. Even Cuban witchc'laft."

Conde looked back to where Manolo was arguing with the guard and then felt the cemetery's unappealing silence. He sensed, as he often did, that his death might be something near and tangible, and he wanted to be far from there. The hypochondriac within started to lash out, and he knew that when that character was aroused, he always ended up depressed or gloomy. *They are really all alone*, he told himself as he lit up a cigarette.

"Here's your man," sighed Manolo as he arrived with the guard, who now walked around the grave and sniffed it as if he were a hunting dog.

"So what do you reckon's in here?" asked the man, intrigued.

Conde didn't look at him but spoke to Manolo: "Call Headquarters and tell them to come and give us a hand. And tell them to keep some slops back for our comrade's piglets …"

The gravedigger's face visibly relaxed. Feeding his pigs must be one of his most demanding daily chores, and no doubt he calculated daily the amount of meat and fat accumulating under the hides of those animals whose eventual respective sacrifice would bring him two coveted goods that were in short supply: food and money.

"If you sort the grub for my five pigs, five, I say, don't worry about anything else. I can open the grave and then get on my way quicker," the guard offered.

"But we also have to look around the shrub they put in the directions for a good reason, because I don't think anyone would hide anything in a *chino*'s grave."

"I do that with spade. Earth soft after 'lain." Juan Chion now offered his services and Conde thought, *There's no way out.* But there always was.

"Fine, get on with it … I'm going to buy cigarettes in the place opposite. I'll be back in a moment." Manolo glanced warmly at Conde before he fled the cemetery.

He crossed the street towards the cafeteria and the first thing he discovered was that the bar next door was closed. Was that a plot at national level? It was just past 5 p.m. and it was ridiculous that the place wasn't open at the best time to have a drink. Yet another? Well, yes, another drop would have done him nicely. What a disaster. He walked into the cafeteria and read from the huge, garish list what was on offer: POPULARES CIGARETTES, LIGHT CIGARETTES, COFFEE. And in the corner, a handwritten sign offered water, with the decisive epithet AT ROOM TEMPERATURE, and he noticed on the other side the bar's becalmed freezer, which could have supplied the whole neighbourhood with water. "Nothing doing," he muttered. "It's a plot." He asked for a packet of cigarettes and hesitated over the coffee. *Do I dare?* He dared, and profoundly regretted it. The would-be coffee left a sweetish taste on his tongue and a few dregs he found almost impossible to spit out.

Conde stood in the cafeteria doorway and looked towards the cemetery. The fence didn't let him see what the others were doing and only the trunk and drooping branches of the weeping willow helped him locate the grave of Li Mei Tang, which must contain, most likely, a few bones, a putrefied coffin, a thousand forgotten dreams and a valuable secret, enough to cost one man his life. He lit a cigarette and looked at the cars driving past. *What might that secret be?* he wondered, not intending to come up with an answer, though he immediately reflected that the person capable of mutilating and stringing up Pedro Cuang must have known Pedro was involved in the gambling racket and had to be the executor of the lost fortune of Amancio the banker, with whom Pedro seemed to have sustained a long friendship and a fruitful association in criminal dealings. And Conde now knew that the deceased had taken his secret to his grave. Or the morgue, where he was currently lying. Besides, the lethal Zarabanda sign had revealed that the murderer was aware of the old secrets of the *mayomberos*, although there was something about that which seemed increasingly fake … And why had they knocked Conde out and not taken his pistol? Perhaps they had just seen somebody come in with a key to the room and had decided to take the opportunity to conduct a fresh search. Or perhaps they had just been taking precautions: perhaps an intruder might find what the murderer hadn't. But if only … *No, no,* thought Conde before he stopped. *They won't fool me,* he concluded, convinced they were only trying to put him on the wrong track with all those clues, hanging a man they thought was dead when he wasn't and who, almost definitely, hadn't revealed the hiding place in the cemetery, for if he had they would have found signs of a search. *But the killer is someone from the Barrio, and I'm going to stop him well and truly in his tracks.* He threw his cigarette butt into the street and breathed deeply until he'd filled his lungs – and over half his *tsin* – with the carbon monoxide belched out by a juddering, packed bus. And when he felt most like getting away from there, he crossed the avenue and followed the path to the grave where the peace of the dead was being disturbed.

When he saw him, Juan Chion shouted, "Hu'lly, hu'lly, Conde." But he didn't hurry. There was plenty of time to see Li Mei Tang's coffin, where only a few bones remained that were probably of no use for a *nganga* (a few ribs and vertebrae; his *kiyumba* was gone), and time above all to be dazzled by what Juan Chion had dug out from the roots of the old weeping willow: pendants, necklaces, rings, earrings and gold coins shone brightly from the inside of a metal box that had certainly cost Pedro Cuang his life.

8

Rufino swam peacefully around his bowl. His fierce fighting-fish fins gently beat the water, driving a circular dance which could only end in the creature's death ... and resume with the arrival of the next Rufino, always identical to the previous one, and to the one before that, and before that, since red fish and the repeated cycles of their lives gave Conde the feeling that something in the world could be, or at least appear to be, permanent and immutable. "That's life, Rufo," Conde told that particular Rufino. "Forever going round in dirty water until we're fucked up. But there'll always be another ready to start the round: until everything fucks up again ... right?"

He sat on his bed and placed his pistol next to the goldfish bowl. "Don't touch it. It's loaded," he warned the fish as he rubbed his eyes. Two days ago, while Patricia had been helping him clean the house, he had pledged to tidy the room properly, but he didn't have the strength to embark on such a task now. He looked at the tower of books piled high on a chair, the original function of which, before he was abandoned by that last woman whose name he didn't even try to remember, had been to provide a prop to daring scenes of lovemaking. The novels he read time and again now slept on that complicit chair. He had been returning to the same books for some time: he knew their characters better than almost all the people around him and felt a strange pleasure when he confirmed that their lives had barely changed between one reading and the next, even though on each reread he discovered different intentions or shades of emotion, because something had in fact shifted, even if it was in a circular movement. He, Mario Conde, had moved, very probably downwards, and it was his new perspective as a reader that allowed him to discover those twinkles or dark places he'd not seen on previous visits to those pages. As if he were a new Rufino in the red garb of the previous Rufino. There was always something set to change in the lives of real, living people. And it was a bastard, and generally was a change for the worse …

Any of those well-thumbed books represented what he would like to have written in another life. He no longer spent too much time thinking about his aborted vocation, though an envelope he'd intentionally mislaid somewhere in his house was the resting place for several stories he'd drafted even against his own wishes. Because he really preferred to live as a parasite on other authors who knew how to write well. *Islands in the Stream*, he read on the spine of one book; *Conversation in the Cathedral*; *Catcher in the Rye*; *Explosion in a Cathedral*; *Horse Fever*; and then he stopped.

Conde prepared the coffee pot in the kitchen and put it on the burner. He was hungry but knew he wasn't in a state to cook anything. And what the hell would he eat anyway? Unless he went out and hunted a *chino* dog in the street with his bow and arrow. He realized the real danger was the nightmares hunger usually provoked. In situations like that, he usually dreamed he went to bars where, for some reason, he couldn't get what he imagined bars should supply, just like in real life. That conspiracy was so well devised it even controlled the world of his unconscious. He drank his coffee and looked out of the window, and reluctantly recalled yet again the last woman he'd had in his bed, the damned woman past whose house he was forced to walk whenever he visited Skinny Carlos. His feeling of abandonment was such he even mouthed her name: Karina. Karina was beautiful, red-haired and played the sax. Was she a real person or had he simply invented her to bring solace to his loneliness? At this point he couldn't say, but he did think he could remember that he'd never made love as he had with that elusive creature, who had become lost in lies, the night and the fog. He threw his cigarette butt out of the window and cursed Karina's mother … That woman had destroyed him in a cruel, brutal, humiliating fashion. *That's the price of falling in love, you fool,* he reproached himself. But he immediately found a sure-fire way to justify himself: *The fact is you always fall in love, Tamara rubbed that in your face, and that's why she's afraid of you, you idiot.* And he thought back to the conversation he'd had the day before with Tamara, to the desire his oldest, most sustained love always aroused, and decided on the spot he needed to see her as soon as possible and, if possible, spark that riveting interaction again.

And that he should kick things off without waiting for her to contact him.

When he returned to his bedroom and laid back on his bed, he reflected how much he wanted to sleep and dream the dream of Cuang Con, that *chino* who had closed his eyes and dreamed he was a butterfly filled with pleasure when he flew over flowers and green fields. In his dream he hadn't known he was Cuang Con, but when he had woken up and was the real Cuang Con again, he hadn't known if he was a butterfly who had dreamed he was a man or a masochistic butterfly who had transmuted into a shitty policeman who increasingly didn't want to be a policeman. As he reflected on the fable of his own erroneous vocation as a policeman without the calling or the talent, he felt the exhaustion, alcoholic excess and blows to the head of the last two days catch up with his body, and he fell asleep. Then he did really dream. But not of butterflies, or even bars. He dreamed Patricia was the naked woman with the jade earrings who came over, caressed him and let him glue his lips to her small breasts and nipples that were as firm and sweet as plums, while his fingers wandered over her infinite thighs before beginning their ascent to stroke the wiry hair of a bush she'd inherited from her mother's black blood. Beyond the entangled mesh of hair Conde ploughed the furrow that disappeared into a deep, mossy well, which his hand, arm and whole body entered, sucked down by an implacable whirlpool. He woke up in the middle of the night, dripping in sweat, viscously damp between his legs, his heart racing. He discounted any idea of going for a shower and fell asleep again. When he woke up, with a sunbeam on his face, it was an effort to remember why his underpants were stiff and smelled of dead *chino*.

Conde would anxiously scrutinize the physical process that, by the mere act of applying heat, made the water ascend, cross the dark powder he'd placed in the strainer and produce the miracle of the liquid that was ready to be drunk. That first coffee in the morning answered the desperate call from his body and every one of his slowly awakening cells. But it only needed the first few sips for his body to begin to settle down: this was catalysed when he took the first drag on his first cigarette of the day. Then, and only then, did he begin to feel he was human again.

The accumulated hunger, alcohol and nocturnal agitation, and the fallout from a bad night's sleep didn't make that morning's Mario Conde feel anything like a thirty-five-year-old man: in fact he felt like he was two hundred, although the cold shower he subjected himself to reduced that horrific figure by half, and the second coffee, with the aforementioned cigarette, restored him to an age even he believed was acceptable: he felt he was down to eighty when he heard a knock on his door and, with his towel wrapped around his waist, he turned the knob and found himself face-to-face with his midsummer night's dream – for real.

"Were you looking for me, by any chance?"

Patricia was in her police uniform and was carrying a bag. Dazzled by that morning vision, Conde reacted in a way he would later deem to be foolish and quite surprising for the sixty-year-old man he always became merely by looking at that woman.

"Where the fuck were you, my girl? You landed me with the case of the dead *chino* and in a flash you'd disappeared ... with a young lad you call your boyfriend and —"

"I did what I promised I would," interrupted Patricia, pushing him gently but firmly out of the way so she could walk into his house. "I spoke to my father so he'd help you and ..."

Conde's ravaged sense of smell detected a second, tempting, unnerving scent. The first, naturally, came from Patricia, who had just had a bath; the second from the bag she was carrying. To his surprise he discovered he was almost back to being thirty-five. A battered thirty-five, but even so, he thought nostalgically when, years later, at almost fifty, he wandered through the Barrio once again, remembering the details of that episode and evoking the energy and illusions he'd scattered on life's path ever since. And above all, remembering that very precise morning when he had fulfilled his dreams ...

"What have you got there?" he asked, trying to peer into the bag.

The *china* smiled.

"I saw the state of your fridge the other day. I can't imagine how you're still alive ... I've come to join you for breakfast."

"Breakfast?" Conde was even more dazzled when Patricia pushed the full ashtray away and started to take supplies from the bag and put them on the table: a loaf that smelled as if it was just out of the oven, a piece of cheese, strips of cured ham, cakes (*coconut or guayaba?*)

115

and a thermos from which she poured two large cups of milky coffee. Did such things still exist? Conde wouldn't have believed it if he'd not seen it …

"Come on, sit down and let's speak," his friend ordered.

Conde thought briefly that he should first get dressed, although he felt very comfortable with a towel wrapped around his waist, his only defence against nudity. Hunger won out, and he sat next to Patricia and started to devour those unexpected delicacies that his stomach joyfully welcomed up to the next dismal moment.

"So what have you found out?" asked Patricia, and Conde, while he chewed breakfast and drank his coffee, tried to tell her about his escapades over the last few days, that had been crammed with setbacks, doubts, mysteries and questions rather than anything concrete. As on the previous day, when he had spoken to his boss, he omitted from his abridged version the idea that Francisco Chiú, Patricia's godfather, might be connected to the murder, although he did add the detail that Pedro Cuang had described the way to find Amancio's treasure in Chinese because he had a specific Chinese recipient in mind.

"And what I most need to say to you …" Conde was nearing the end of his account. "From the very beginning I've felt that your father knows something he's not telling me. Something that might be important if I'm ever going to solve this case."

"What do you think that might be?" asked Patricia. She was listening hard and had barely touched her (*coconut!*) cake or coffee.

"Aren't you going to eat your cake?" Conde enquired, trying to sound casual. She shook her head and pushed the plate over to him. He grabbed it as if it might run away. "You know, I don't have a clue … but I think Juan knew Pedro Cuang better than he's letting on, and that his friend Francisco, your godfather, also knew him, and very well at that."

Patricia sighed so deeply it shocked Conde.

"Mayo, I'd like to thank you for what you're doing … Anything that's related to my father is too important for me …"

Conde listened and said nothing, and decided to keep it that way for once. It was clear that Patricia wanted to talk.

"I can't claim he's been the best father in the world, but he's better than anyone you could have dreamed of having. His family always came first. He emigrated to Cuba to find a way to support the family he had as a child and worked like a mule all his life for his family here and I …"

Patricia had touched on a spot that was too painful and no doubt too sensitive, because as she spoke her voice began to fail and her eyes moistened until two tears rolled down her chocolate cheeks. Conde was subject to many frailties, including the inability to watch a woman cry: he simply collapsed before such a spectacle. Consequently he dropped his cigarette, went over to Patricia and caressed her braided curls, which were silkier than he'd imagined. Softer than the pubic hair in his recent dream.

"It's all right," she said, and she tried to smile as she took Conde's other hand. "There are so many things, my father …"

She gave Conde's hand a friendly tug, which was enough to cause the towel around his waist to fall to the floor like a theatre curtain. Patricia saw an erect penis hardly twenty inches from her nose, pointing at her like a water pistol ready to shoot. Conde moved to retrieve his meagre fig leaf, but Patricia squeezed his hand and stopped him. Conde gulped and looked at his stiff appendage, which was fortunately all of thirty-five and had been rejuvenated by the unexpected breakfast.

"I swear by my mother I wanted to console you … but I couldn't stop thinking of that something else," said Conde, his sincerity also stripped naked for her to see. "The truth is that whenever I see you, I can't stop thinking about that other thing … Whenever. And you know …"

Patricia smiled.

"Oh, I thought all that business about laying a Chinese mulatto was a game you were playing …" The woman's irony verged on sweet talk while she squeezed Conde's hand harder and her eyes looked up into Conde's or down at his reddened, already dripping glans.

"I never toy with such things, or turn down a coconut cake, or invoke the name of the Lord in vain … I bloody —" Conde started to say and almost jumped into the air when the back of Patricia's hand brushed against his scrotum. But when the nails of that same hand ran up the smooth underside of his penis, his trembling legs exploded in a shudder that penetrated his anus, burned his nipples, dehydrated his brain and left him completely defenceless, only fit to reduce the few inches separating his aching penis from Patricia's face.

He was fainting, he was fainting, he thought when he felt the warmth of Patricia's lips, her tongue and mouth wrap round his weepy but erect creature. No, he wasn't

118

fainting, he was dying … Conde felt he was ascending to heaven, even hearing St Peter's keys jangle, or was it the ironware of Congolese Zarabanda or Lucumi Oggún? So what if it was? That was heaven, for fuck's sake, pure heaven.

An hour later, after fulfilling so soundly at such a random moment one of his life's most persistent desires, Conde boiled up more coffee and poured a cup for Patricia, who'd slipped her officer's uniform back on: the kind that imprisons and interrogates. Mario Conde was convinced that erotic act would lead nowhere and that he should simply accept it as the magical consequence of the fortuitous descent of his towel and human frailty, though he also knew he would never again look at Patricia with the same eyes: he now knew at first hand, had seen, tasted, even penetrated what her clothes concealed. He had tangible visual material to embellish his dreams and masturbatory sessions.

Conde sat down on the other dining-room chair with a fresh cup of coffee and lit a cigarette.

"So, Patricia," he said, clearing his throat. "What must I do to get old Juan to tell me what he doesn't want to tell …?"

Patricia tidied her braided curls and drank her coffee.

"Mayo, I don't know what my father knows, although you *are* right: he does know something. They always know something, but they never let on …"

Conde snuffed out the cigarette he'd been smoking.

"Please, Patricia, don't you start being all mysterious too."

"No, Mayo, I'm not being mysterious … Let me finish, for heaven's sake. Look, first, I want to remind you of something you know only too well: my father, Francisco, Pedro and all these *chinos* are men who have paid the highest price for existing in this world. They have experienced the worst: they have starved, been insulted, discriminated against, uprooted and everything else you want to put on a list of lousy experiences and humiliations. You ought not to be surprised if they're suspicious and don't open up just like that."

"I understand what you're saying," Conde allowed. "And that's precisely why I've been trying to track you down and talk to you for the last two days. I'm afraid that by attempting to find out the truth, I might hurt more people who don't deserve to be. Your father, for example. I've a nasty feeling … Or Francisco Chiú, your godfather, who has a role in all this too, though I don't fucking know what."

"Francisco is dying," she responded. "Liver cancer."

"Your father told me he was in a bad way, but not …"

Patricia looked him in the eyes. And Conde got the message at once: the lieutenant knew something very big *she* didn't want to let on. Something that Conde needed to know in order to have some idea of what he was into and how much shit he might uncover.

"Tell me, Patricia," he ordered.

Patricia didn't stop looking into Conde's eyes until she started to talk: "My father told you the story of his cousin Sebastián, the one who wanted to go to California …"

"Yes, the one they froze and chucked into the sea."

"Sebastián and thirty-one other *chinos*. It was a massacre."

"Hell … And if he'd had the money, your father would have been in that boat," said Conde, while he prepared himself for her revelation.

Patricia took a last sip of coffee; it was cold by now.

"Yes, he and Francisco. Because one of my godfather's brothers was also sailing in that boat. That's why Francisco saw the Greek captain the day his brother signed the deal with that bastard … Like he saw the captain again here in Havana, drinking a beer in a bar as if nothing had happened, twelve years later. By that time everyone knew what they'd done to those thirty-two *chinos* in the Gulf of Honduras. I suppose that a drunk sailor must have bleated what happened and that's how the news spread and reached the Barrio … When Francisco saw the man who'd killed his brother, he didn't think twice: he decided to take his revenge. My godfather, a greengrocer at the time, always carried a knife on him, but misfortune is writ in the most ridiculous ways: on that day he didn't have a knife because he was going to the Jewish tailor's on Calle Muralla to buy a suit for my parents' wedding. So when he saw the Greek, he rushed back to the Barrio to look for his knife … and bumped into my father. Francisco was furious, he was acting like a lunatic, but he didn't tell my father what was wrong or what he was intending to do … That day my father should have been working at the grocer's, but by chance the delivery boy was ill and he had to do the errands around the Barrio. That's why Francisco and my father met. The moment my father saw his friend, he realized something serious was up, and almost forced him to tell him what had happened. And finally Francisco *did* tell him … and my father left what he was doing. They both went to look for a knife and then went to look for the Greek bastard who should never have come back to Cuba … And they found him."

Conde felt the huge weight of that story fall on his shoulders – a delayed but justified revenge: an execution. And was speechless.

"My mother found out straight away," Patricia continued, "but she also kept the secret. Thirty years later, she told me, just before she died. She decided to tell me because Francisco's son was in prison and my father had asked me to help him and I had refused, saying that if he'd done something wrong, he should pay for it … My mother didn't know what had happened after Francisco and my father went to find the Greek captain, although you hardly needed to be an oracle to guess. I even researched it afterwards and found it reported in one of the sensationalist newspapers of the time. People suspected the Greek had been killed in a drunken brawl … But what my father and his friend had done together was so terrible their relationship became much deeper and complex than simply friendship: something that can only exist when you have killed a man, right? … That's why Francisco Chiú is my godfather and Panchito is my father's godson …"

Patricia was silent and looked into the coffee dregs in the bottom of her cup as if she could read there the key to a fate that had put her father in a street in the Barrio Chino when Francisco, on a day when he hadn't been carrying a knife, had been returning home to find the revenge weapon, a set of coincidences able to lead Juan Chion to the murderer of his cousin Sebastián.

"The past is the past, and now think of it as never having existed, although you know it existed and what its ingredients were …" Patricia seemed to need a pause to gather her breath, and then she concluded: "The present is what's important. Solve the case of Pedro Cuang, Conde."

"I'm going to do just that, Patricia."

"But try to make sure there isn't much collateral damage, as my father said you told him … The poor man looked the word up in a dictionary … I know what you're like, and that's why I asked Major Rangel to give you the case and promised him that my father would help you …"

The *china* finally smiled again as she got to her feet and, with a sad smile, gently caressed Mario Conde's face. She turned round and went into the street, removing from Conde's reach the vision of that edible woman … that he had now devoured at least once in his life. Down to her last fibre. Like a juicy melon in the month of May.

9

Fatty Contreras looked him up and down and smiled. Recently everyone was seeing him in a different light or laughed when he came into sight, Conde reflected, and put out his hand to be tortured: one of the favourite pastimes of Captain Jesús Contreras, head of the Currency Trafficking Section, was to unload the pressure from his two hundred and sixty-five pounds into a handshake.

"Conde, oh Conde," he greeted him, as he always did while he crushed the lieutenant's fingers, and, as he laughed, he pulled on Conde's hand and led him into his office. "Hey, you feel really soft today ... and your face is a bit odd ... you're kind of pink ... What *did* you get up to this morning?"

Conde smiled.

"I can't say ... but it was something fantastic."

Contreras gave him a more leisurely inspection.

"I know what it was, what I don't know is with whom ... Although if I made the effort, I'd find out soon enough." He smiled again with his whole body, as usual. "Yes, when you have a good one in the morning, it relaxes you for the rest of the day, right? Come on, out with it, what's on your mind?"

For years Conde would remember that man's encyclopaedic insights, and, above all, the way his whole body shook when he laughed, the way the voluminous architecture of that police captain's flesh shook, a man who months later would be demoted, fired and tried for continuous, hefty major crimes of extortion, brought to light by the still secret investigations in progress that Major Rangel had alluded to without revealing the slightest detail. Who would have thought at that point that Captain Jesús Contreras, the smiley, easy-going fatso, ever efficient and helpful, was a corrupt policeman whose actions even put on the line the head of Major Rangel, the honest officer who unfortunately acted as his boss? Twenty years later, whenever Conde evoked the image of Fatty Contreras, the by then ex-policeman, he felt an uneasy mixture of disgust, gratitude, anger and compassion for the defenestrated fraudster.

"I've got a dead *chino* on my back, Fatty," he'd said that morning, when Contreras could still be a lifeline.

"Well, I know a *babalao* who's wonderful when it comes to getting rid of the dead and prying spirits. He must be good if he has clients who come from abroad for the ceremony when they're mounted by a saint and pay him in dollars … He's a real eccentric, because he's Ukrainian, of Jewish extraction, and became a *babalao* here in Cuba. What do you reckon? Obviously, it's the Government that draws up his contracts with these foreigners and pays the Ukrainian *babalao* in Cuban pesos … Ho-ho. What do you think? Just tell me and I'll fix you a time so he can give you a good clean-out?"

"Don't piss around, Fatty. I'm in a foul mood and have got a *babalao, palero* and *abakuá* who's streets better than yours …"

"And does he get paid in dollars? Tell me, because if so, I need to put him inside this very minute for currency trafficking …"

Conde sat in a chair in front of Captain Contreras's desk and glanced around his office.

"So don't you offer your pals a coffee any more?"

Contreras laughed, but it was a short-lived eruption.

"So you'd like a coffee? You don't know that orders from above reduced rations and I don't get any any more." While he spoke he walked round his desk and flopped into his armchair. Conde always wondered the usual – *how does that poor chair stand it?* – while he watched the show Contreras put on before giving him his coffee. "You tell me how the fuck Walesa and his bloody Poles are connected to the yuccas and sweet potatoes planted in Matanzas? Or Gorbachev and his load of shit to coffee from the slopes of Guantánamo? A shipyard fucks up in Poland or the Soviets start eating shit, and there's no sugar here or I lose my coffee ration …"

"Forget the coffee," suggested Conde, while thinking Contreras was right. But that was hardly the moment to discuss the global socialist economy or the future of communism in Europe. Or in China.

"Well, just take a look here so you can see I love my pals," the captain continued, opening a desk drawer and waving his huge paws over its contents like a magician over his hat: he took out a glass of coffee and handed it to Conde.

"Hell, it's even hot!" exclaimed Conde, as if shell-shocked.

"I kicked up such a stink that to shut me up Major Rangel sends me a glass whenever they slip him some coffee, because, of course, they didn't touch *his* ration ... A matter of hierarchy, right?" And he let loose a laugh. His flab, tits and bottomless barrel of a belly danced to the deafening rhythm of his guffaw.

"Nobody can touch you, Fatty," responded Conde, though life would show him to be wrong. Who could claim that Contreras wasn't a nice guy? Who knew he was more than met the eye?

"And that's even though people here are always mouthing shit about me. And you know that's true, although you don't, because we're pals, right?"

"Well, you know, it's exactly that: I swear I can't live without you."

"Naturally, that's why you're here. Out with it: what's getting to you? By the way, does the dead *chino* on your back have anything to do with the live Chinese consul who was in Major Rangel's office this morning?"

Conde shut his eyes. That was all he needed.

"The Chinese consul?"

"That's what Rangel's secretary told me ..."

Conde lit his cigarette; it had never even crossed his mind that the inhabitants of the Barrio Chino were at all connected to the consulate of the country that wasn't the same country that they had left, even though, luckily or unluckily for them, *chinos* would always be *chinos*, even if they had surgery to change their eyes. He realized he had to speed things up and got straight to the point: he was there because he needed Captain Contreras to let him have a snitch.

"Someone who knows all the goings-on in the Barrio Chino, Fatty: what's cooking, what's the gossip. I'm sure you must know such an individual."

"Oh, really? Easy as pie, right?"

"Help me, Fatty. This is a complicated business, you've seen how even the embassy's got involved … and take a look at what they did to me yesterday." Conde turned his head to show Contreras the contusion at the base of his skull.

"That was some whack," Contreras replied, not laughing now, and added, "No, we can't allow this … It shows a lack of respect and —"

"But they didn't steal my pistol. Does that make any sense? How much is my pistol worth right now?"

Contreras pondered for a few seconds and declared: "Rented out, with eight bullets, a hundred pesos a day. Sold, like three thousand, because lately there's been great demand …"

"So they rent them out now, do they? I didn't know that. You need to help me, Fatty."

"That's the second time you've said that."

"And I'll say it a third: help me, *compadre*."

"All right, man, I'll throw you a lifeline … You know, you're a straight-up guy and there's not many of those around these days. But let me remind you of something: never start thinking you're better than everyone else. We're all wading through shit here and nobody escapes unscathed, nobody ... I defended you when you had that fight with Lieutenant Fabricio, because Fabricio is a fuck-wit and it was time someone kicked him up the ass and did him over ... But I know you sometimes give yourself airs, you play the intellectual, and that pisses off lots of people. When you're police, you've got to behave like it and not get above yourself, because a policeman who's disliked by other police is in for a very hard time ..."

Conde let him ramble, as he was interested in Contreras's view, which he found somewhat surprising.

"And what's the point of that spiel right now, Fatty?"

"The point is that this place right now is a time bomb and it's best not to decide to start running when it blows up ..."

Conde recalled Major Rangel's mysterious warnings about drugs, and was sure something serious was cooking beneath the apparent routines of Central Headquarters for Criminal Investigations. And, as on so many occasions, in so many places, he felt an overwhelming desire to clear off to the remotest back of beyond.

"I'll give you the best operator I've got in the Barrio."

He was almost knocked off his chair by Contreras's voice. The other man's finger was pointing at his face like a plantain. "But take good care of him. Narra is worth a million pesos. And only use him on the case you're investigating now, don't mix him up in anything else. I know you only too well when you get going ..."

Evidently Narra must be part Chinese, which was why he was called Narra, the name given to all Cuban *chinos* for some damned reason or other. This Narra revealed his origins particularly when he laughed: his eyes became two deep furrows in his face, symmetrical fissures with a sombre, sinister allure. He didn't look *chino* in any other way, though: more like your average mulatto, fished out of a trunk of memories. He sported a *démodé* flat-top with tight curls and no sideburns, the hairstyle that had characterized the smart-asses and wheeler-dealers of the 1970s, and the dark skin of his right arm bore a tattoo that announced, "Eva, I'd die for you". *What could Eva have done for him or given him that he was so ready to die for her?* Conde thought he should ask. Narra's smile revealed two dazzling gold teeth, like yellow reflectors. "Let him laugh as much as he likes," Contreras had warned him, "but the fact is he shits himself the second he sees a cop." Narra was thirty and had spent twelve of those years in jail, first for robbery with GBH, then for dealing in illegal currency, and that was how he had fallen into the lap of Fatty Contreras, who had worked hard to break him in and had got his sentence reduced in exchange for certain services. "Treat him well," the captain had added. "He'll be expecting you at 1 p.m. in his sister's house in El Cerro."

When Conde flashed his lieutenant's card, Narra laughed sarcastically, as anticipated.

"I'm a friend of your friend Contreras," the lieutenant told him, and Narra let him in. His sister lived in the premises of an old grocery store on Calle Cruz del Padre, whose fate had been changed: first by the government law controlling food supplies, and then, out of necessity, transforming it into a gloomy, soulless abode. Conde noted one room, a kitchen and a bathroom before Narra told the woman who was cooking, "Cacha, I ain't here" and pointed the policeman to the stairs to the wooden mezzanine floor they'd built thanks to the very high ceiling and where they'd installed the bedroom.

Conde felt like he was visiting a prehistoric cavern. *Why do I keep getting into this kind of shit?* he wondered, and went upstairs to find a completely unexpected space: all kinds of electrical equipment for every possible use glinted in that improvised bolthole, a spot which betrayed unexpected economic potential that revealed the strongest inside protection in a range of forbidden ventures. But he remembered Contreras's warnings.

Narra offered Conde a chair with a battered seat, before sitting on the edge of his bed.

"They're going to roast me, Lieutenant. Contreras is putting on the pressure. This area is red-hot at the moment."

"You've nothing to worry about. Nobody saw me."

"They miss nothing around here. The street's full of eyes."

"Don't get worked up," said Conde, trying to calm him down. He could smell the fear of that fierce-looking guy who'd entered into a pact with the devil.

"The police never lose," came the reply, and Narra took the cigarette Conde offered him. He looked for an ashtray and put it on the floor between them, within easy reach. "If anyone cottons on that I'm snitching for you, I'll be straight off to heaven. You do realize that?"

"I can imagine ... Though I'm not sure it would be heaven ... But I needed to talk to you today."

Narra looked at his nails: he had long, thick nails, sharp as razor blades.

"So what do you people want now?"

"It's easy enough. Did you hear about the *chino* who was strung up in the rooming house on Salud and Manrique, three blocks from here?"

"Yes, everything gets out. And if it's a *chino* who's been hung ..."

"That's precisely why I'm here now. What are people saying about it in the Barrio?"

Narra took a puff before replying. "Not much, just that they strung him up."

"I reckon they weren't intending to, but the situation got out of control. They were looking for something they apparently didn't find, because they came back ... Was that fellow involved in the coke that's around in the Barrio?"

Narra avoided Conde's gaze, and the policeman took the opportunity to observe his informer's hands: they had a slight tremor, but it was more sustained and visible than anything fear might cause. *Cold turkey?* Conde wondered, and regretted having promised not once but twice to restrict his questions to his search for the murderer. Narra finally spoke as if what he was saying wasn't important.

"Naw, I don't think so. That consignment left the Barrio some time ago, all there is now is a bit of marijuana ... The people selling charlie to tourists are suicidal and you never see them around here ... No, not with that shit ..."

"But people here are saying the *chino* had Amancio the banker's money. What can you tell me about that?"

Narra was definitely far too nervous. He stubbed out his half-smoked cigarette. Conde knew the man had a history of violence and aggression, but now, when he saw how his hands were shaking, maybe at the idea he might be discovered by others who were equally violent and aggressive and might have power, he pitied him. *I'm too soft for this shit,* he thought. *How long am I going to be stuck in this rat trap?* The idea of using his own position of power to apply force to a man to make him bend and shake in fear or wish to escape also degraded him as a human being. But it was assumed he must do that job, re-establish order, shed light on mysteries, find a murderer ... and his sarcasm, which seemed to upset so many, was the personal resource he used to protect himself. And conversations like these were the nefarious means he often had to resort to on behalf of a socially necessary end. *It's shit all the same,* he thought.

"You never leave anyone in peace ..." his snitch finally mumbled.

"Forget that and tell me what people are saying round here ... And remember: it's better to have two friends than one, and I know how to repay a favour." Conde felt himself slip several rungs down the ethical scale simply by uttering those words. *As I said: shit and more shit.*

Narra took a deep breath and flung himself in at the deep end.

"Well, about a month ago I heard some gossip in the domino school that sets up next to the barber's that's part of the San Nicolás store. About that *chino* having Amancio the banker's loot. If it's true, it must have been a lot, because Amancio was a real mover and shaker ..."

"Uh-huh. Who mentioned Amancio's money?"

"Naw, it was the riff-raff in the Barrio, and they were drinking … Pissing gossip."

The snitch kept nervously fingering his tattooed arm. Conde remembered he should ask about the virtues of Eva. But later.

"Narra, don't beat around the bush. Tell me who it was."

The snitch patted his jeans pocket and Conde got the hint: he took out his packet and offered him a second cigarette. Narra needed to plug nicotine into various holes gouged out by fear.

"Panchito," he said, after lighting up. "But he was blathering, I think he'd smoked a toke tube."

"A toke tube?"

"A doobie, a spliff, a blunt, a weed joint …"

Conde took a last drag on his cigarette and prepared to ask *the* question. He hoped against hope that the imminent reply wouldn't be what, inevitably and fatally, it was bound to be.

"Who's Panchito?"

"Panchito Chiú. He lives up the top of Lealtad. But, as I said, that guy is a professional fucking big mouth. He always carries a *chino* knife with him and says he's an eighth-dan karateka …"

"A karateka?" rasped Conde, feeling the bottom of his skull, which was still sore. A contusion to be added to a long list of collateral damage he could see coming.

"Yeah, he spends his whole time talking big so people are afraid of him, and now he's a high priest and always bragging that Changó is protecting him and all that shit, but the guy —"

"Yes, you said: he's a fucking blabbermouth … I'll give your regards to Captain Contreras," said Conde, getting to his feet. He didn't need to know any more. He didn't want to know any more. Not even about Eva. Then he wondered how he should say goodbye to the snitch. *Should I thank him?* he wondered. "Thanks for everything," he said in the end and was about to shake Narra's hand, but decided not to: the canary's hands were still shaking and must have been sweaty. He was already carrying enough shit, on top, inside and out. And a canary will always be a canary.

He was now in a position to gauge the severity of the error he'd made under Patricia's insistence: he should never have forced Juan Chion to get mixed up in that business. But then he remembered the matter of collateral damage and better grasped what Lieutenant Chion was up to: the *china*, who must have suspected where the shots were coming from and even had other fears she'd not confessed, must have reckoned it was preferable for the case to fall into Conde's soft hands and not the claws of another detective. And that breakfast with coconut and guayaba cakes, followed by her succulent body, had perhaps been part of her scheming. Would Patricia, a colleague, have dreamed up such a tactic? Was she asking him to cover up, rather than expose something, and had she done so using every one of the weapons in her armoury? No, Conde couldn't believe that. But at the same time he couldn't stop thinking about it.

He came out onto the street and neither the bright sunlight nor the image of Narra skulking behind the door, staring at the ground as he headed outside, annoyed him, because Conde felt he'd been forced to profane a grave he should never have touched. Troubled by business that included dead from the past and present, but above all disgusted with himself and his inability to grasp people's motives, he crossed Calzada del Cerro and walked to where he knew Manolo was waiting for him in the car. As usual, the lieutenant felt he was on the verge of solving the case, yet the thought didn't bring him any cheer. On the contrary, he sensed the job was coming to an end and leaving in its wake a long and painful trail of shit.

It was no surprise: unless he radically changed his life, another sordid job would always be waiting around the corner. Then he turned an actual corner and made a V sign when he saw Manolo: the unfortunate Pedro Cuang's murderer wouldn't be free for much longer, because even if it wasn't Panchito, he would lead them to the snake's tail. Or was it its head? And what if, as he thought, the criminal *was* Panchito, Juan Chion's godson? Well, Panchito would be up shit creek: guilt must be paid for. If not, someone should go down to hell and ask that bastard, the Greek captain, who liked to freeze *chinos* and throw them overboard. But ... which *chino* had been meant to get those cemetery directions?

"I think we fucked up badly," he blurted, almost without thinking, as he got into the car.

"How did it go?"

"In the Barrio they reckon Pedro Cuang had Amancio's inheritance, or knew where it was, and that a Panchito Chiú was pretty interested in the old man's money. What's more, the guy always carries a knife and is a *palero*, and would know the Zarabanda signature … And as you can imagine, this Panchito Chiú is Francisco Chiú's son, and it wouldn't be too much of a coincidence if the shadow of that giant cat we saw in the Chinese Society was his, would it? I think the clever ruse of branding old Pedro and cutting his finger off is going to cost him dear. Divine punishment for playing games with Zarabanda, right?"

Manolo drove by the Cerro stadium: the cathedral of baseball in Cuba. Conde looked down one of the open passageways between the terraces and caught a fleeting glimpse of a ground that was so green and peaceful, now empty. He recalled the countless occasions he'd sat down with Skinny – when he was still skinny – Andrés, Candito and other friends of theirs on the terraces of that sanctuary of soil and grass where the magic rites of the sport (if it could be called that) were practised. The last time had been barely two months ago and with the very same friends, Skinny Carlos included. When Conde stepped inside that magnetic place he felt released from the tensions of life, a freedom that only came with the build-up of other tensions inspired by a good game of baseball. The championship had finished two weeks ago and he was still suffering from his team's inexplicable defeat; they had collapsed in the final straight after leading from the start of the season. *Those pansies ought to have won*, he thought, remembering how devastated Skinny had been after their three-month dream of glory had been dashed in just one horrible week.

"Balls, they don't have balls!" Carlos had shouted, and he had been so right. It was all a matter of balls (*or rather a lack of …*).

When they came out on Calle 19 de Mayo, Conde looked at Manolo: "How many useful fingerprints were found in Pedro Cuang's room?"

"Seven."

Conde put his hand in his trouser pocket and extracted the envelope containing San Fan Con's wooden rod.

"See if any match the ones on here ..."

"Are you saying that Francisco Chiú —"

"I'm not saying anything ... But I do believe that if Panchito's prints are among those found in the room, he won't even need to confess. And you know what? I hope they aren't his. I hope what I'm thinking isn't what happened ... Even if I have to spend another week on this case, and have to learn to speak Chinese, eat with chopsticks and join the Long March ... I hope it isn't him and that his father isn't involved in any way ... For old Juan's sake ..."

They drove up Ayestarán, crossed the traffic lights on Carlos III, and turned onto Calle Maloja. Juan Chion's house was still there, crushed by its neighbours, "until death do them part".

While Conde knocked on the door, Sergeant Manuel Palacios repeated the inevitable rite of unscrewing the radio aerial and putting it inside the car. Those streets were capable of robbing even police. "Let him take his precautions, Conde, that's not your business," the lieutenant muttered as he banged the knocker hard and waited to see Juan Chion's smiling face.

"Oh, police," he said, and invited them in.

"Why you in such a sweat, Juan?"

"Exercise, Conde. You should t'ly some. Look, you skinny, but you got a belly on you."

"And I've got news … Bad news, I reckon," he paused, before throwing the stone that would trigger the avalanche. "It looks as if Panchito Chiú, your friend's son, is involved."

Juan Chion looked at Conde and then at Manolo. Any remnant of a smile disappeared from his face and drips of sweat ran slowly towards his neck. The old man slumped into his battered chair and sighed, as if he were deeply in love. *A painful love*, thought the lieutenant, for whom that part of his history was dead and buried and who was now enjoying the advantage of being able to read the signs.

"See, Conde, why I didn't want to be in this? *Chino* searching misfortune of other *chino* …" he said, getting to his feet.

Juan walked further into his house and Conde stared at the photo that always occupied pride of place on the small table in the centre of the room: Juan Chion didn't have any grey hair and was smiling happily at the camera. He was carrying a toffee-coloured two-year-old girl with *chino*esque eyes that had been enhanced with make-up. The little girl was wearing the shiny dress of an Eastern princess and only her skin colour and curly hair cast doubt on her Asian origins. A woman was standing next to Juan Chion, and she and the girl were holding a fake diamond-and-emerald crown that rounded off Her Highness's outfit. She was a beautiful black woman with exuberant hips and sturdy, sculpted legs, and she too was smiling for the camera. The print could have been called "Happiness".

Juan Chion came back carrying one of his pipes. He sat back in his chair and said: "Misfortune b'ling misfortune.

Chino shouldn't meddle where he not wanted. I learned that a thousand years ago," he said with a cryptic reference that was now as clear as daylight to Conde, before closing his eyes and inhaling. He took the pipe from his lips and the smoke slowly escaped from his mouth, as if it was abandoning him for ever. Conde felt excluded from old Juan Chion's grief and reflected that his work usually brought that kind of lousy reward. "Shit work," he muttered, took another look at the photo and opted for the patience of Job, as they say.

He wasn't overly surprised by Juan Chion's fresh revelation that his journey to Cuba had been financed by his old friend Francisco Chiú. He had purchased the permissions and boat ticket so Juan could flee Canton's appalling poverty and start a new life, perhaps a better one, on that remote Caribbean island. The *chinos* thought such a gesture had eternal worth, because it represented a defiance of individual fate and, at the same time, created for each of the protagonists responsibilities and obligations that lasted for the rest of their lives: Francisco became like a father to Juan, who, in turn, owed perpetual gratitude to his benefactor. Was it that burden of gratitude or the fate of Sebastián that had made up Juan's mind to accompany his friend the day they had gone to kill the Greek captain? Conde would never know, although he believed the horrendous death of a loved one must have prompted Patricia's father's drastic decision.

The friendship between the two men was much more than social convention or moral obligation, much more than an affinity through being born in the same

Cantonese village or having played in the murky waters of the same river and knowing they descended from warriors who had fought with Cuang Con to free the women of their realm. It related to what was unutterable, painful and forbidden. That's why they had tried, with the joint baptisms of their children, to seal the bond from the blood they had spilt: in their eyes that commitment before a God that was new but one they accepted had a single clear meaning: the godfather is a second father and the godmother a second mother, and that was what they had pledged on that afternoon in front of an altar in Havana.

Panchito's mother had died first, and his father, working long hours in the grocery store, had no time to look after his son, who was brought up on the street without the advantages enjoyed by Patricia. And that was what most worried old Juan Chion: he was the father of Patricia, whose mother had brought her up with so much love and integrity, while his second child, Panchito Chiú, hadn't had the same opportunities. And now, to top it all, he'd participated in the outcome of an investigation whose climax would not have a happy ending … The news would kill Francisco, Juan had declared, and Conde remembered the Tao philosophy and the paths for humanity Juan Chion himself had told him about: wasn't each child's path written before they came into this world? Patricia was the good one, the intelligent policewoman with a cunning streak, as was right – or as, according to prejudice, she should have been as a result of her Chinese genes. The other was the murderer, the hoodlum, stupid and garrulous to boot … *Shit, nobody, not even San Fan Con, believes in that predestination rubbish,* he answered himself and, without looking into the old man's eyes, tried to find an excuse.

"You didn't do anything fate wouldn't have done anyway. If it really was Panchito, we would have eventually found him out, my friend. And remember that he killed a fellow countryman of yours and his reasons for doing so. I feel sorry for his father ..."

Conde gestured to Manolo. They got up and, as the lieutenant walked past the old man, he rested a hand on his shoulder. The *chino* barely batted an eyelid.

"Some jobs are like this, my friend. Look after yourself. Do your exercises ..."

"Come back another day," said Juan Chion before he shut his eyes and took another puff on his reed pipe. "If you see Pat'licita tell her to come quick." Conde felt that old man's sorrow touch his own heart: Juan Chion didn't deserve to suffer from guilt and blame that wasn't his. Not even if it was marked out by the irrevocable destiny of his *tao.*

10

Manolo signalled to Conde, who finally spotted him: Panchito Chiú came out onto the sidewalk opposite the Lung Con Cun Sol Society, looked both ways and walked towards the corner the lieutenant was patrolling.

After comparing prints and seeing that Panchito Chiú had been so good as to leave them a little present in the form of several of his all over the rope from which Pedro Cuang was hung, Conde decided he'd make the most discreet arrest possible, accompanied only by Manolo. That's why they'd been waiting for the past two hours for the guy to leave the building, thus avoiding any feline transmutation or Bruce Lee-style rooftop chase. The wait, and exhaustion, had given Conde a parched throat and an aching back. He observed the young man's elastic gait – the bastard really did seem a bit of a cat or tiger – and he remembered how Narra had warned him about Panchito's knife and the fact that he liked to boast about his mastery of the martial arts. Besides, the way he'd silently entered Pedro's room and struck him without the lieutenant noticing his presence demonstrated the man's physical prowess. For a moment Conde regretted the habitual sloth that had led him to abandon the gym after only his second self-defence class in order to hide in his office and read a novel which brought joy to his life and reignited his desire to write. The self-recriminations lasted two seconds: Panchito was ten yards away, and Manolo was walking ten yards behind the young man. Conde took out his ID card and shouted: "Halt: police!"

Conde saw the youngster's muscles tense with alarm. Panchito looked over his shoulder, saw Manolo closing off his retreat and seamlessly passed his arms over his chest to adopt an attacking stance: as if by magic, he was already holding the gleaming tip of a long dagger in his right hand, ready to throw it. For a moment Conde imagined a cinematic miracle would come next: he even felt like his backside was seated comfortably. Panchito would lightly flex his legs and, propelled by special effects, would fly up before the eyes of his police audience and land on the roof of the Society, and from there he'd make another flying leap and be lost in the mists of the Barrio Chino. But Panchito Chiú was your average *chino* and didn't enjoy such filmic powers. Conde was disappointed by this, but more disappointed that the young man was threatening him with a dagger.

"Hey, don't be so fucking stupid and drop that knife," Conde shouted.

"Come and take it off me," the karateka retorted defiantly.

"Look, lad, I told you to drop it. Don't make life difficult for me, it's already lousy enough," Conde almost implored him. "Be so good as to drop it, and —"

"What's wrong? You scared?"

"Drop that damned knife, for fuck's sake!" bawled Conde, as if all the energies in his body were coming together.

That shout surprised the youngster, and Conde, who always thought things through, did so now despite his state of mind: *Better not take any risks*, he told himself, and *Right, I am scared*. Then he took out his pistol and, also seamlessly, aimed at the knees of Panchito, who'd recovered from his shock at Conde's outburst and was now brandishing his knife, ready to attack. Conde didn't give it a second thought: he fired. When the bullet hit Panchito Chiú, he dropped the dagger and fell to the ground, rolling around and howling like a wounded dog. It was the second time in his career that Conde had shot someone, and he did the arithmetic only after pulling the trigger.

"Fucking hell, Conde, you're crazy!" shouted Manolo, as translucent as rice paper, not budging from the spot assigned to him in that drama: right behind Panchito. "What if you'd missed this idiot and put a bullet in me?"

"Well, they'd have pinned a medal on your chest, Manolo. But I'm sure that this little son of a bitch who almost knocked my head off yesterday is so out of his mind that today he was quite capable of throwing his knife at me." Conde wiped the sweat from his brow, tried to bring his shaking hands under control and, after kicking the knife away, walked over to the wounded man – who was still howling, but the cop needed to let off steam – and bawled at him again, "Was that what you were looking for, you little shit?"

11

"So what are you doing here at this time of day?"

Conde looked into her eyes. His mind was full of thoughts, ideas, projects, recriminations, but he lacked the precise response she wanted and was only able to say what every cell in his body was proclaiming: "I feel ill ..."

Tamara eyed him for a second and decided he wasn't lying.

"Come in and take a seat ..."

The reaction that had led him to Tamara's house had been visceral and irrepressible. The fact that he'd had to shoot a man, even though he tried to do the least damage possible, had gone against his natural instincts and invalidated him as the human being he was or was trying to be. That was why he had asked Manolo to take the case forward and had fled from the hospital where they'd driven Panchito Chiú and, almost not knowing why, had turned up at the house of his dreams and stood opposite it contemplating but not seeing the concrete sculptures with their shapes halfway between Picasso and Lam for more than twenty minutes before deciding to knock.

No sooner had he sat down and watched Tamara go to get him a glass of water, he realized he'd begun his recovery: he couldn't stop gazing at her buttocks and reflected that, rather than water, the ideal beverage would have been a drop of that Ballantine's, the last dregs of which he had drained on his previous visit to that house.

Tamara gave him his water and offered to make coffee, but he asked her to sit down. Then he told her: he'd shot a man.

"Obviously I didn't kill him, Tamara. I wounded his leg, nothing serious," he added, seeing how alarmed she looked.

He lit a cigarette and stared at her. Now he knew why he was there: not because of his rejection of violence, nor to avoid hospitals and interrogations. At that moment he needed an anchor, a support that not even his lifelong brothers, Carlos, Andrés, Rabbit and Red Candito could offer. Nor the red-hot sex of Patricia, or Karina's wild eroticism. It was something more intangible but more vital, more profound.

"I've almost had no time to think about what you said to me, but at the same time I've been thinking about it non-stop," he said, immediately lamenting his awkward formulation.

"And what do you think you think?"

"I don't only think about you. Most of all I think about myself. About the shit I've done and am doing with my life. I think about loneliness, and how it frightens me. About how I can't put off any longer trying to sort out what can still be sorted … and I think how it would help me a lot to do all that with you …"

Tamara looked down and wiped the palms of her hands across her skirt as if she needed to clean the sweat off.

"What exactly do you mean, Mario?"

"That I need you ... Damn, that sounds like a bolero ..."

"And are you by any chance thinking that we should get married or something?"

"No, I've not got that far ... Or, yes, I have, to be frank, but the idea scares me," he said, and felt like smacking himself: there are things you should never say to a woman. "But that's not what's important. The other stuff is important."

"The other stuff?"

"Having you near me ..."

She stared at him again. Conde could almost hear the cogs turning in her mind.

"Mario, don't ask me to sort your life out now. First I need to sort out my own ... And I'm going to be frank too: I sometimes think you're part of the process, but I'm not sure."

"So what do you need to be sure?"

"Time. Give me time. And don't pressurize me, please. I know you're an obsessive-compulsive type, but give me time ..."

Conde looked into her eyes: they were two moist almonds, as ever, and he understood, or thought he understood the woman's plea.

"I must go," he said, standing up.

"You're not annoyed with me?"

"Well, a tiny little bit," he said and then smiled. "But don't you worry, take your time ... I'll be back tonight to hear what you've decided ..."

"You're the most insufferable guy I've ever known."

"I had to be the best at something, didn't I now?"

He couldn't stop himself; he raised his hand and stroked her hair. And thought: if he was going to make the mistake of getting married again, it would definitely be to that woman. And, sure, he could guarantee it would be all for love.

"So?"

"Don't worry. The bullet barely grazed his skin and didn't damage any bones. The fact is he was shit-scared when he saw things were getting serious. After they'd dealt with him, I showed him the fingerprint results, and he told us everything. He says old Pedro must have had a heart attack and died in his arms, apparently from fear or rage when Panchito strung up his dog to pile on the pressure ... Panchito had been so agitated he hadn't realized Pedro had only fainted. That was why he decided to string him up from the ceiling. He swears that there was nothing but papers and junk in the room and that he took nothing. Obviously, Amancio's money had been converted into jewels and was in the cemetery ... He thought up the Zarabanda ploy on the spot. Ever since becoming a *palero*, he'd kept the two tokens in his pocket – he says they brought him good luck – and then he carved the cross into Pedro's chest and cut his finger off so people would think it was do with voodoo or revenge rather than money. The worst damned part was that I had to listen to his story for almost an hour because he was so confused ... he was crying," said Manolo, handing the folder to Conde.

"What about the fingerprints on the San Fan Con rod?"

"They're in the folder as well."

Conde opened the folder and looked for the analysis of the prints. It confirmed what he'd suspected. Then he took out the sheet of paper and the envelope with the rod.

"Manolo, do me another favour," he asked as he handed back the file. "You take this to Major Rangel. I want to go and see Juan … What news have you got of Lieutenant Patricia?"

"She left a message at Headquarters to say she was on a case, but nobody knows where she's got to …"

"Forget it, I can imagine why that bitch's not around … She can take care of herself. I'm going to try to take care of the things that concern me … It's the time of year for putting things to rights … Oh, and tell Major Rangel that Pedro's death isn't connected to drugs and that the case is closed."

Conde walked down to the Headquarters' parking lot and asked the duty driver to take him to Infanta and Maloja. On the way, the new recruit who was driving tried to start a conversation about his ambition to become a real policeman, but he soon gave up when he saw his audience's complete lack of interest. The lieutenant was smoking and looking out at the street, and everyone at Headquarters – even the greenest recruits – knew what that meant. "Better not talk to him … He's a pain in the neck," said some, although most added: "But he's a good guy."

"Should I turn down Maloja, lieutenant?"

"No, drop me on the corner, it's right there. Uh-huh. Thanks, Rosique. Oh, and think it through. This isn't a good job ... Why not be a mixologist?"

"A mixologist?"

"A barman, the kind who mixes the drinks their customers want ..."

Conde relished the expression on the rookie's face and waited for the car to drive off before finding the right way. He walked a block and, when he turned down the first side street, he saw him: heading away from him, towards the other corner, Juan Chion walked with steps that seemed to have lost their usual elastic spring. Conde put away the sheet with the fingerprint results and the envelope containing the rod. He took out a fresh cigarette and his dark glasses and started to follow the old man. Initially he assumed he was running household errands, as he was carrying a shopping bag. But after they'd walked six blocks, he started to grasp what was happening. They crossed Carlos III and it was crystal clear: the old fellow was walking towards the Barrio Chino. He was walking unhurriedly, at a steady, sustained pace, only stopping to cross roads.

Juan Chion turned down Zanja and walked towards the centre of the Barrio. *What's he up to?* the lieutenant wondered, keeping some fifty yards behind his unexpected prey. From his confident perspective as a poacher he began to feel a tangible sense of shame in a way that might overwhelm him. He had no right to spy on old Juan Chion's private life, especially at a time which must be really painful for him. But he was curious to find out what the *chino* was going to do and persisted in his pursuit.

By now they had walked almost twenty blocks and Conde was beginning to feel like his poor, stretched metatarsi were on fire, while sweat was running down every crevice of his body. "I'd bet a cigarette he turns down Manrique," said the lieutenant, and paid himself with one of his meagre Populars when the old man turned down the street where the late Pedro Cuang used to live. *But what the fuck does he want?* he wondered, and hurried to catch him entering the tenement. However, Juan Chion only stopped for a second in the entrance to the rooming house, surveyed its gloomy interior and then carried on walking. *He's going to the Society*, Conde thought, and that was why he had to trail him beyond the Restaurante Pacífico, beyond the Chinese newspaper, and watch him turn into San Nicolás. When Conde peered round the corner to see where he presumed Juan Chion's long journey would end, he found himself eyeball to eyeball with the old man.

"So you like good long walk, Conde?" the *chino* asked, and Conde begged the earth to swallow him up, immediately, right there in the middle of the Barrio.

"My friend, the truth is …" He tried to find an excuse, but couldn't lie. "I needed to talk to you and was surprised to see you leave home. I don't know why, but I decided to follow you."

"Walking good exercise."

"Yes, so they say. I meant to tell you … I don't know … I meant to tell you something …" The policeman was embarrassed, and was unable to tell him what he now knew or to express the solidarity he also needed to communicate to the old man. "You going to see your old friend?"

Juan Chion nodded and glanced in the direction of the entrance to the Lung Con Cun Sol Society.

"I owe him explanation, 'light?"

Conde took off his glasses.

"I think so. You two are always going to have a lot to talk about … But you're not to blame for what his son did, and I'm not —"

"It not about blame, Conde. You silly. Look: it g'lief and shame. Panchito killed one of our count'lymen and … shame also kills, Conde."

"All right, I get you. Talk to him, but don't feel guilty …" Conde thought hard again, wondering whether he should throw into the hat the piece that would complete the puzzle of Pedro Cuang's death, and though he thought it was cruel, he also thought it was right, and even necessary. "Look, Juan, I wanted to see you because there's something I've not told you that I'm not going to tell anyone else, but I *am* going to tell you now. So you don't feel guilty about anything at all …"

"What's that, Conde?"

"Your old friend, Francisco, knew all about Pedro Cuang's money, and the cemetery directions were most certainly meant for him. Nobody has told me this, and I don't want anyone to tell me either, but I'm sure Francisco told his son that the money did really exist and that there were directions … and that's when the rot set in."

Juan Chion looked at some vague spot behind the policeman.

"And how do *you* know all this?"

"Because Francisco's fingerprints were all over Pedro's room, because Francisco was Pedro Cuang's friend, because Francisco can read Chinese, and because Francisco is Panchito's father and Francisco knew what his son was involved in ..."

"And you certain you told nobody else?"

"Not even Patricia."

Juan finally looked at Conde and, after a long silence, whispered, "Thank you, Conde." The *chino* held out his right hand and Conde shook it. Then he took from his shirt pocket the envelope where he'd put the San Fan Con rod he had used to compare Francisco's fingerprints with those found in Pedro Cuang's room.

"Look, give this to Francisco." He handed the envelope to Juan. "Tell him I'm returning it so the curse of San Fan Con doesn't fall upon me ... And now I'm going to take my tune elsewhere," said Conde. "And forgive me for following you."

"Naw, I understand, police stuff ... Oh, and if you see Pat'licita, 'lemember to talk to her. She 'lespect you, Conde. And she c'lazy, c'lazy ..."

"Don't you worry, she's not crazy at all ... Anyway, I've got lots to tell her too ... Come on, I'll walk with you that far," he said, putting his arm around Juan Chion's shoulders. "Although it's all ended like this, I've enjoyed working with you, my friend. One learns things."

"What sort of thing?"

Conde thought: that you *chinos* are still very peculiar, that there really is a *chino* smell, that honour and friendship are friendship and honour, that revenge never brings back the dead and that parents are never able to be objective about their children, whether in Cuba or China. But he said: "That *chinos* are not little ants."

Then Juan Chion stopped and took his hand.

"Conde, Conde, you know well, shame kills. Do you know the shame I feel, and Pancho as well? Yes, you do … You good man. I've done ho'llible things in my life, and don't 'leg'let anything, I don't." The old man was insistent about his lack of regret, and Conde thought that in fact he was filled with regret; lots of it. "Because there things you must do in life, 'light?"

"I understand, Juan. And don't regret anything. Sure, there are things that you have to do at some point in life … and others you shouldn't."

"T'lue … Goodbye, Conde, go home," the *chino* interjected, and gave a small bow.

Conde stood still on the sidewalk and watched him go up the steps to the Society. At about the tenth step Juan Chion's figure disappeared into the darkness, as if he had levitated to the remote and peaceful world of Cuang Con and his warrior brothers. Before setting off, the policeman took out of his pocket the sheet of paper with the results of the fingerprint test on the rod, tore it into several pieces and dropped it through the grating over a drain.

He walked back to the corner, trying to shed his woes and fill up on futile consolations that, fortunately, Juan Chion hadn't let him express, and then he noticed it again: that *chino* smell. Of course: it was a warm, persistent, yellow smell. At least the smell survived in that barrio with its past full of sordid stories and its moribund future, that magical barrio where, as if risen from a daydream, he found an open bar, ventilated by huge ceiling fans and packed with bottles of rum.

He immediately entered the place and went to the polished wooden bar, sat on a stool and rested his elbows in front of him. A mulatto mixologist came over, wearing a dazzling white shirt and a white bow tie.

"What's up, Conde? The usual?"

And the policeman nodded and didn't worry about the dream coming to an end.

The mixologist took a bottle of Santiago rum from a shelf behind him and placed it on the bar. He picked up a gleaming glass and dropped in a small ice cube. Conde enjoyed the sound of the ice against the glass and was about to ask the mulatto to do it again. The discreet mixologist poured rum over the ice until he'd half-filled the glass with that wonderful glinting liquid and, not saying a word, with the gift of discretion not possessed by Cuban barmen, he withdrew to leave that man alone to ruminate over his obsession with his favourite tipple.

Feeling refreshed and tranquil, Conde took his first gulp and understood how direly his *tsin* needed to be immersed anew in alcohol. *Just as well anything is possible in this city*, he told himself on that summery afternoon in 1989, when he was still a policeman and was suffering as a result. He took another swig and prepared not to allow himself to be banished from that paradise found as he had been expelled from so many others, real or imaginary. He would drink in his ideal bar until rum brought the relief of oblivion. When it shattered against reality, he'd have time enough to think about his *tao. After all*, he told himself, after his third assault on that glass of rum and ice, *there are things that nothing or nobody can change.*